Lipstick LIES

KRIS BUTLER

Lipstick
LIES
KRIS BUTLER

Contents

For the past five years, I thought I knew, without a doubt, what had happened the night my life had been turned upside down. As it turned out, I might've been wrong.

Faced with the truth, I have two options: believe Ryker and let go of my grudge, or continue to run from reality and pretend everything was okay.

I was tired of pretending.

Joining The Order hadn't been part of my plan, but it might be the only thing that saved me now. I had two weeks to see if I had what it took to join their ranks.

And then… I'd take down the *real* enemy.

With my men at my back, I would show the world just how deadly lipstick and stilettos could be.

It was time for Finley Reyes to save the day.

Foreword

Join Finley in this spy-esque why-choose romance that will contain dark themes. This is the final book in the duet and intended for readers 18+ and older due to adult situations and content.

This is a spin-off of The Council Series, but it isn't necessary to read first. Some characters will cross-over, enriching the experience, but aren't required to know in order to enjoy the story.

This book contains light MM and can be skipped if desired (marked by the author).

This book contains violent situations and themes. There is an active shooter situation, as well as mild torture.

Sometimes it takes a while to find your voice. Never stop trying, no matter how many walls you have to knock down, or times you fall. Your voice matters.

SHE EMERGED in a red dress and the shoes I'd sent to her. The heels clicked against the pavement as she walked across the parking lot. She moved with such freedom and optimism that it instantly made me want to squash it out of her.

And tonight, I'd get to do just that.

I'd been preparing for this over the past six months. At first, I assumed she'd flake out like all the others had and leave me to my mission. But Finley Reyes had proven to be more persistent and annoying than I'd bargained for. Especially when she started to encroach on *my* territory. I couldn't let her stand after that.

So, I waited and devised the perfect plan, infiltrating from the inside.

She pulled her phone out of her bag and I watched as she tapped into the app. One of my monitors lit up, showing me her message. I currently had three screens visible as I worked. One featured the app, logged into three different accounts after I'd cloned theirs, the middle displayed the video footage of Oblivion, and the last was the actual account we were hacking into.

Focusing on the first part of the sabotage, I responded to Finley from the cloned account.

Oblivion: I'm here. Are we set?
Blackhawk: We're all good. Ready on your count.

Switching monitors, I silenced the alarm for the school Finley was at and disabled the one for the true test back to back. It was a lot to manage all at once, but I'd been preparing for this night for months and I was ready. Every step had been outlined in my notebook of when and what I needed to do so I wouldn't accidentally screw up my chances to get into the MidKnight Guild while I thwarted Oblivion. If tonight didn't go as planned, I'd have to try a different approach. But with everything meticulously scheduled to the minute, along with my skills and expertise, it should all go off without a hitch.

A message popped up on the actual server, and I clicked over, triple checking I was on the right one. I'd even colored-coded each one to distinguish them apart and keep them separate. It would only take one stray message sent to the wrong person to screw it all up. Not that there hadn't been close calls in the past, but everything hinged on tonight's mission.

Blackhawk: I'm in position. Alarms?
Obsidian: Good to go.
Blackhawk: Any update from Oblivion? She should be here by now.
Obsidian: Nope. Guess she couldn't hack it in the end. Being grounded is a rookie move and not an excuse if you want to be a Knight.

I wanted to laugh at my joke, but there was no one here to hear it, so I chuckled softly to myself, enjoying my own humor.

Blackhawk: I thought she had what it took. Keep trying to get a hold of her.
Blackhawk: I'm in. Going silent.

The need to punch something rose up in me at his words, and I calmed my breathing, remembering it would all be over after tonight, and he'd be mine, once and for all.

Obsidian: Everything's clear. You got it.

Quickly, I zoomed back over to the other monitor, checking in on Finley. She walked toward the main office, not even realizing the alarm was going off the whole time. I snickered at my ingenuity as she set her own trap. Loading some pre-written text, I added it to the voice app for it to say. I'd already set it to wait a few seconds between each voice and change the octaves on the voice manipulation to help distinguish between us.

The most amazing thing to come out of this past year was the tech that I'd created. Finley had been a big help to motivate me to design something I could use to manipulate her. I'd even gotten off on the fact she'd developed some of the specs. I didn't know what that said about me, but I also didn't care. I'd use whatever advantage I could to get ahead.

I was twenty-one, had spent most of my life alone, and had finally found what I was good at. I wouldn't apologize for going after what I wanted at whatever cost. Too many people had discarded me, used me, or dismissed me over the years for me to have any empathy for others. The world was brutal, and the sooner she learned that, the better off she'd be. In fact, I was helping her understand the world before she let too much of her optimism out. She needed to buck up and see the world for what it truly was.

And now that I knew what I was good at, I didn't want anyone else coming in and stealing it. There was only one person I cared about, and I wouldn't let him be swayed by an underage girl who thought she could steal him from me. This was an act of kindness that I was doing for both of them.

Blackhawk: I got the files. Can you make sure the cameras are wiped? I'm headed out.

Obsidian: Already done. See you back at home base.

Blackhawk: Still nothing from Fin? Maybe she got caught on her way out?

Obsidian: Nothing. It's probably for the best, anyway. She never even realized we were all in the same city. How good of a hacker could she be?

Blackhawk: That's not fair. We concealed our location on purpose.

Obsidian: We found hers. She should've been able to do the same. We can talk about this later.

Blackhawk: Fine. Losing both Mongoose and Oblivion. It just feels like we failed.
Blackhawk: At the bike. Going off.

I watched as he mounted his bike, knowing he wouldn't drop this anytime soon. I'd have to be vigilant about making sure she wasn't able to reach out. I needed her to hate him. Good thing I'd already planned for that with the gifts and messages.

As the red and blue lights flickered on the monitor, the last piece of my plan fell into place. She'd have a hard time contacting us now. I knew she'd been picked up before for minor things, but there wasn't a judge in the state that would let her off the hook for breaking and entering. If only I'd thought ahead of time about pinning Mongoose's murder on her. Then I really wouldn't have to deal with her.

He'd been a liability I hadn't seen coming. Oh well, in the end, he'd gotten himself killed. I only wish I'd had more time to prepare so I could've used it more to my advantage.

As they escorted Finley to a police car, I began to wipe the clone accounts and closed out all the tabs I had opened. The tracker on Ryker's phone alerted me to him arriving, so I finished up all the back-end things as I waited.

When the door to our room opened, I spun

around and smiled as he entered. Standing, I walked over to him, picking up the bottle of tequila we'd been saving. I couldn't stop the smile from spreading across my face.

"I think a shot is in order?"

He peered up at me, sighing. "Let's get it all submitted first. I don't want to count our chickens too soon."

Rolling my eyes, I set it down and spread out all the information we'd collected over the past year. This was part of the initiation we hadn't shared with Mongoose or Oblivion either, leading me to believe he hadn't wanted to from the start, planning on cutting them out, to begin with. It was only because Oblivion turned out to be a girl that Ryker had changed his mind.

"What do you think they're going to do with it all?" he asked.

I shrugged my shoulders. "Does it matter? We were asked to find information on some safe houses, troubled kids, and organizations that could be exploited. We have it. Now, we turn it over."

"I know, but it feels wrong." He peered up at me, and I saw the doubt that had been creeping more and more into his eyes reflected there.

"This is everything we've been working on for the past two years! Don't fall apart on me now. We'll be rich and have more power than we could've dreamed of. This is it, man. Just think of all the things you can buy. The freedom of never being hungry or worrying about which bill to pay this month."

Ryker sighed, dropping his head and letting out a long breath. He raised it after a few seconds, a smile spreading across it. "You're right. I've just been distracted. This is it. No more worries."

We scanned everything in and hit submit. I ignored how he hesitated when he entered the team members present for the last test. Once it was final, he scooted back, grinning.

"Shot time?"

"Shot time."

Picking up the bottle, I poured us both one, and we tapped them together before downing the liquid. It only burned slightly and we laughed at the feeling. Sitting on the ground, we passed the bottle between us, toasting our success and the things we planned to do with our money once our tech went live.

"I want the freedom to walk into almost any store and just be able to be like, yes, I want that and not have to worry about it," Ryker said.

Scoffing, I moved closer to him, falling as I went to grab the bottle and landed on his shoulder. "You can do better than that. I want a flashy car and a house with so many rooms, I forget about them."

His hand brushed mine as he grabbed the bottle, and I blamed the tequila for my lack of inhibitions. My love for Ryker wasn't anything new, but doing something about it was. Combined with the success of the evening in both getting rid of Finley Reyes and passing initiation for MKG, I decided to take my chance.

Leaning forward, I pressed my lips against his. He didn't move away, so I took the opportunity to push harder, my tongue sweeping out to ask for entrance. When he opened for me, I cried joyfully and pressed further, owning his mouth like I'd always wanted.

Things escalated quickly as we both got naked, rolling around on the ground, the empty bottle of tequila next to us. Reaching down, I pulled on his hard cock, knowing I wanted it more than anything else.

We didn't say anything as he plunged into me, the pain of the intrusion lasting for a moment before he was pumping with drunken movements. Neither of us lasted long, spilling out onto the floor, adding to the spilled remains of our shot glasses. Ryker rolled over, a snore leaving him a moment later, and I soon followed, too high on the success of a job well done.

I'd gotten everything I wanted in one evening.

Ryker. Money. Prestige.

Which meant that it all had to fall down around me in the morning leading me to transfer schools.

But I never forgot Ryker. If anything, my obsession for him only grew, and I vowed to become so powerful he'd never be able to push me aside ever again.

Ryker would be mine or no one's.

One

FINLEY

WHEN MORNING CAME, I stayed still, not wanting to face the day. I'd been awake for several hours now but hadn't moved. Everything felt heavy, and I wondered if it was the drugs… or me.

Someone had gotten up a while ago, but I was too focused on myself to figure it out. I'd been held in a pair of arms all night. It was the only thing that kept me from falling apart. My mind kept replaying three things.

Blackhawk had a name, and it was Ryker.

Ryker was the leader of The Order and Cohen's handler.

He claimed he hadn't set me up.

I'd heard them talking as the nurses hooked me up to the IV, but I hadn't wanted to believe it. I'd been able to push it off until this morning, but I would have to face it soon. Suddenly, the thought of knowing the truth seemed like the last thing I wanted. What if everything I'd thought for the past six years had been a lie? Where did that leave me then?

I'd never felt so lost in all my life.

"Babe, I can hear your thoughts running a mile a minute. I promise, whatever is said, I'll be there to help you figure it out. We've got this. Together."

Asa's soft words soothed me, and I relaxed for the first time in hours. Carefully, he turned me, bringing me to face him. It was then I realized that we were the only two people left in the bed.

"Hey," he said, tracing his thumb across my cheek. "How are you feeling?"

Licking my lips, I swallowed, wetting my dry throat so I could speak. I was too worried to care about morning breath. "Physically? A bit tired, but otherwise, I think I'm okay. I feel so embarrassed that I passed out."

"You went into shock, Fin. It was more than passing out. You don't have to be so hard on yourself all the time."

"It's the only way I know how to be," I admitted, closing my eyes. "It's easier than letting others do it."

"I don't think you really believe that," Asa whispered, pulling my chin up. My eyes naturally opened at the move, finding his green ones. They were so full of hope, love, and reassurance that I wished I could bathe in them. "What are you worried about discovering?" he asked when I didn't contradict him.

"That the past six years have been a complete joke and waste of time. Everything I thought I knew was wrong, and I'm nothing but a failure." Tears began to build, threatening to spill over my eyelids. Saying it out loud felt different than it just running around in my head.

Asa pulled me closer, his body practically wrapping around me as he held me to him. He dropped kisses on my eyes, nose, forehead, and hairline as the tears began to fall.

"You are magnificent and the furthest thing from a failure, Finley Reyes. You show me every day what it means to be strong. You strive for your best, showing others they can too. You care deeply for people, almost to the detriment of yourself, and you're always willing to be there for a friend. You're the most selfless person I know. If that is what a failure looks like, I want to be a failure too. But you haven't failed, my love. Not at all. Sometimes we just have to take a moment to readjust. Absorb the new information and recalculate our next move. It doesn't mean the last effort was worth anything less."

Peering at him through my tear-filled eyes, I grasped ahold of him, needing to feel his solid presence. The moment my hand touched him, I felt something settle, anchoring this man to me.

"I'm so glad I found you, Asa. You're a dose of pure sunshine combined with the strength of an unwavering force. I love you so much."

Gently, I pressed my lips to his, knowing I wasn't ready for anything more this morning, but I needed that small connection to remind me that I had him.

Asa pulled me to his chest, and I lay there, crying as the morning sun began to fill the room. At that thought, I realized we were underground and there shouldn't be sunlight coming into our windows.

"Wait, are we still at The Order?" I drew back, taking in the room. It looked like the same place I'd brought my bag to yesterday.

"It's artificial sunlight," Cohen said, and I turned toward the door, finding him watching me. When he saw I was looking, he came closer, sitting on the end of the bed. "How are you feeling?"

"Tired, but otherwise okay. What do you mean artificial sunlight?" I asked, sitting up. Asa followed, the cover falling and reminding me of his gorgeous chest of muscles. My hand lifted, and I realized I was about to pet him. Clasping it in my other hand, I dropped them onto the bed and looked at Cohen. He smiled at me but took pity and didn't comment on my near groping.

"Since a lot of the people here don't go up top a lot, they had screens made that mimic the natural environment." He got up and walked over to the wall where the curtains were drawn halfway over a window. There was a remote on the sill, and he picked it up, pointing it at the window, or I guess, screen. "You can set it to whatever time zone you like, part of the world, and season. Some people get tired of winter, so they have it set to more of the east coast and get all the seasons. I just have it on neutral, so it mimics what is outside the building."

"Wow, that's some smart tech. I bet it does wonders for people stuck down here for long periods."

"It's reduced a lot of seasonal depression. There are even sunrooms where people can go and get vitamin D."

"Oh, that sounds cool. I wouldn't mind checking it out. Could we do a tour later?"

"Absolutely." Cohen smiled, sitting back down and practically petting my foot under the blanket. He sighed, his face changing, and I knew I needed to check in with him. "Ryker called to say he'll be here in about thirty minutes. So, now's your time to grab a shower if you want one." He'd practically gritted out that last part, confirming my suspicions.

"You know what?" Asa started, looking at me before glancing back up. "I don't think she should be alone. You should join her to monitor. I want to check out the weight room, so I'll grab one later."

Cohen swallowed, watching me. Smiling over at Asa, I squeezed his hand, knowing he'd seen the same emotions I had and was giving me this time with Cohen to make sure he was okay. Climbing out from under the covers, I crawled over to Cohen. His face lit up at the gesture. I forgot that his confidence was a mask for his insecurities. I leaped, falling into his arms, taking a chance to see him smile.

He stood up, swinging me around with his momentum. Laughing, I held on as he carried me to the bathroom. I peeked over his shoulder, finding Milo watching me from the small kitchen area. I waved, offering him a small smile. He seemed to relax at the gesture, and I decided if I was going to make this work, I needed to spend some one-on-one time with him too.

Cohen sat me on the counter as he shut the door and turned on the light and fan. He set about getting the water ready before turning and looking at me. "I'll just sit out here in case you need me."

His cheeks were red, and I couldn't fathom what was embarrassing him. "You're not suddenly being shy, are you, Co-bear?" I batted my eyelashes at him, reaching for his hand.

"Co-bear?" He laughed, coming toward me, keeping his head down.

"Yeah. It's like Care Bear, but Co because you're Cohen. It's dumb. I'll find another nickname for you."

"No, I like it." He peered up finally, his hands moving to bracket my face. He sat his forehead against mine, closing his eyes as he breathed me in for a minute. "I was so scared I'd lost you, Fin. Everything happened so fast, and then you were on the ground. I'm so sorry that happened. I had no idea that Ryker was Blackhawk."

"It sounds like there's a story there. Let's get in the water before it runs cold, and you can tell me about it."

He gulped, his eyes opening. "You want me to join you?"

"Yeah." I smiled, pushing back as I lifted the shirt I was wearing over my head. His eyes dropped to my breasts, and he stepped back, quickly removing his clothes. I hopped down from the counter and slipped my panties off. I couldn't help but take in every inch of Cohen as he discarded the last of his clothes.

His cock was already jutting out as he eyed me. Taking his hand, I stepped into the shower, realizing how small it was when we were both there. Laughing, I stepped under the water as I took in all the ways his muscles dipped. I spotted a few tattoos, and I couldn't wait to check them out more. Our first time together had been so spur of the moment that I hadn't been able to fully appreciate the gorgeous specimen that he was.

"You're hot, Co-bear." I couldn't be sure under the water, but I could've sworn that his cheeks heated more. "Hand me the shampoo."

"Let me wash your hair?"

Smiling, I nodded and turned around. Softly, he began to massage the shampoo into my hair, taking care of each strand. I wasn't surprised when he started to talk. Cohen seemed to be the type that needed to be doing something when he shared deep things.

"Seeing Ryker was a shock to me yesterday. I hadn't seen him face to face in a few years. In fact, I'd actively been avoiding running into him. It seemed to work, as he didn't seek me out either. Which, of course, relieved and infuriated me at the same time." He made a noise that sounded like he was letting out a breath as he turned my head, massaging different parts.

"Ryker was the first guy I felt anything more than just a passing fancy toward. We went through training together when we were of age and instantly hit it off as friends. We were inseparable there in the beginning. We did a few missions together and worked on projects. My sexuality had always been a bit of a mystery to me. I'd experimented with both guys and girls, but nothing ever felt right. Then I met you, and it felt like my heart was on fire, so I assumed I was hetero. The label didn't feel right though, but I couldn't deny how you made me feel. So when I started to feel attracted to him, it took me by surprise. I tried to deny it because I didn't know what that would mean. One night, he made the first move when we were hanging out by kissing me."

He paused, dipping my head under the water before turning me, his eyes snagging mine with heat, but there was more there than just lust. Cohen held so much emotion in his eyes that it made me reach out to him, wanting to protect him from whatever he was about to share. He didn't stop me but grabbed the washcloth and began to soap it up. He started to wash me in soothing gestures before he spoke again.

"In my gut, I knew it was just a fling for him. He had a reputation, after all, but I thought I was different. It was both the best and worst relationship of my life. When it ended, I took a leave of absence and did some freelance jobs. When The Order reached out to me, I said I wasn't ready to return to the facility. They brokered an agreement that I didn't need to return, except once a year for annual training and a physical. I was also told I had a new handler and that they would communicate only through text or email. I wouldn't need to meet or do any check-ins. It felt like the best way forward, so I accepted."

He'd carefully washed me from head to toe while he spoke. He grabbed some conditioner off the shelf and held it out for me, asking if I wanted it. I nodded, and he turned me back, putting it in my hair.

"Since then, I haven't kept a serious relationship, my heart too battered to try again. I kept flirting with you online, which was enough for a while, but I wanted more. That night, I was going to ask you, finally having the guts to do it, only to find out you'd been kidnapped and had a boyfriend. But then the crazy thing of belonging with that group happened. Sawyer's relationship intrigued me, and I began to feel part of me coming back alive again. At first, I thought about stealing you from Asa, but he turned out to be a great guy. Then it felt like there might be a possibility for me, but I wasn't sure how to get it. I'd almost given up trying, wanting you to be happy with Asa and not interfere with that when you left again. My heart couldn't take losing you, so I went to Asa, planning on only helping him find you and then disappearing."

I sucked in a breath, turning to look at him. "You were going to give up?"

"Yeah." He nodded, sadness in his stance. "But I couldn't ever walk away. I kept telling myself, after this, or after that. I'd planned to walk away that moment in the hotel room when Asa arrived. But then I had to finally admit that I didn't want to. Asa and I had talked, but I wasn't sure how much of that was just him wanting to find you and saying whatever it took to make it happen. Hope speared me when he seemed to be upholding his words, and I knew I was a goner. I know it's too early for you, but I love you, Finley. I have for years, and I just wanted you to know before it was too late."

I pulled his face down, needing to kiss him after he'd shared all of his heart with me. He was right that I didn't know how I felt about him yet. I cared about him a lot, but I didn't think I was at the love stage yet. So, I was glad he wasn't expecting me to say it. When we pulled back, I held his head close, wanting him to hear everything I had to say.

"I can't say those words yet. But I know I will, one day, if you give me a chance."

"That's more than I ever dreamed of." He lifted me up, my legs going around his waist. I could feel his hard cock against my stomach, and I rocked against it as he moved us toward the water so he could rinse the conditioner out.

"Fuck," he cursed, almost stumbling as I did it again. "I wish this shower was bigger so I could show you what happens to naughty girls, sweetheart."

I sucked in a breath, biting my lip, wanting to know what that was. But he was right. This shower was too small, and we'd be more likely to fall and hurt ourselves than enjoy it.

"How do you feel about Ryker now?" I asked when he set me back down, so he could wash his own hair really fast.

"Probably the same as you," he said, giving me a knowing look.

"Like you want to smack his face but kiss it simultaneously?" I asked with a laugh.

"Yep, that sounds about right." He shut off the water, pulling open the curtain. Cohen stepped out first and grabbed a towel. "The one nice thing is I finally figured out what I am. Talking with your brother and Soren helped me with it. I think I'm a pansexual. It's more about the person and my relationship with them."

"Oh? I can see that," I said, trying not to moan as he carefully dried me. "You know I accept you no matter what, right?"

He peered up, some lightness seeping in. "Yeah, babe, I know. Thank you for that, though."

"So, what do we do now?" I asked, wrapping the towel around me as he dried himself. The arousal was starting to climb again, and I knew if we didn't get out of this bathroom soon, I was about to say fuck it and let him have his way with me up against the counter and make Ryker wait for us.

"I guess we hear him out and then go from there. As my handler, I trust him and have a bond I can't describe. He was also a good friend before things ended romantically with us. I don't know if I could forgive him or trust him again in the other area though."

"Yeah, I know what you mean. We had a good relationship online, but then he hurt me. I don't know how I'll feel if that's brought to a different light."

"Well, the only way to know is to find out. Come on."

He pulled me out, and we both dressed in the room. I popped back into the bathroom and quickly dried my hair, putting on some makeup. I wouldn't usually care, but it felt essential to have it on with Ryker coming over.

It wasn't to look nice. Nope. It was to feel invincible.

Yeah, we'd go with that.

I'D BEEN EATING the same bite of bagel for the past five minutes. Chewing it to the point that it was basically molecules. The conversations I'd had with Cohen and Asa had been good for me, but it didn't change the fact that I was about to face the man I blamed a lot of my shame on.

"Would you like some tea or coffee?" Milo asked, drawing my attention.

"Yeah, sure. Coffee would be nice." He smiled, standing, looking pleased to have something to do. He set a mug down in front of me a minute later, fixed precisely how I liked it. I shouldn't have been surprised, but it seemed Milo kept shocking me.

"Wow, that's perfect. How did you know?" I asked, needing something else to focus on more than the need to know.

"I pay attention." His cheeks tinted a smidge, and I smiled at the effort.

"Well, thank you. I appreciate it." I took another sip, liking having something to do, so I searched my brain for a new topic that didn't deal with me or my drama.

"So, where will you be starting your residency?" I asked, keeping my fingers wrapped around the mug. The warmth and familiar gesture were both grounding me.

"Um, well, I'll actually be working in the health clinic at Lux Brumalis. The doctor there is leaving, so I'll be starting in his place. I'll be supervised by one of the doctors at the hospital in Salt Lake."

I gulped, burning my throat in an attempt to not spit out the hot liquid. In hindsight, it might have been better than scorching my esophagus.

"Oh, wow," I coughed. Trying to relieve some of my throat's pain, I grabbed the glass of water and drank it down. The cool liquid felt nice on my throat, and I breathed a sigh of relief. "Sorry. That took me a little by surprise. Um, can I ask what made you pick Lux?"

His cheeks went full-blown red, his ears even turning pink at the top. "Um, well," he sputtered, rubbing the back of his neck as he tried to find the words. "It just seemed like a nice place, and the opportunity came, and I thought I could do with something less stressful."

"Have you worked with athletes before? They're high maintenance," Asa bellowed, his laugh filling the space.

"Yeah, well, it will be a good learning experience. I think Utah is nice."

"Just admit you did it to be closer to Fin. We won't hold it against you… too much," Cohen teased, picking up his tenth piece of bacon.

"Oh, um, well…" Milo began to mutter, and I took mercy on him.

"No matter the reason, I'm glad you'll be closer. It will be nice to get to see you more and spend time together. If that's what you want, I mean."

"Oh, yes. I'd like that." He seemed to finally find his words and stopped his stuttering with my proclamation, and I felt things might be okay with us. A knock at the door had us all tensing as Cohen got up, taking the few steps toward it.

I watched as he took a few deep breaths before squaring his shoulders and opening the door. He stared at the man on the other side for a moment before stepping back and gesturing for him to enter. Ryker stepped in, and my body reacted. The man I'd met at the bar, who'd made my insides flutter, was standing right in front of me. It was hard to reconcile him with the guy I knew online who had broken my heart.

His intense eyes watched me, scanning from top to bottom, almost like he was checking me over. It wasn't sexual at the moment, but more of an assessment of my physical well-being.

"How are you doing today, Fin?" he asked, that dark and delicious voice bringing goosebumps to my skin.

"Better, thank you." I hadn't meant to sound so curt, but it rolled out of its own violation.

"You look beautiful," he said, and I only stared at him, lifting my coffee.

"I know," I finally said, not knowing why I was being so rude. He smiled, making me think he liked my sass, and I pushed that aside. I didn't need him to like anything.

"Should we gather around the couches? It might be more comfortable," he offered, gesturing toward the furniture.

Sighing, I acted put out to have to move, taking my cup of coffee, I rose and walked over. I sat in the middle, Asa and Milo on either side, and I felt safe. Cohen remained standing, leaning against the wall, ensuring we were protected from all angles.

"What do you have to say for yourself, *Blackhawk*?" I said, narrowing my eyes at him. I wouldn't make this easy for him. He had a lot of explaining to do, and I wasn't going to let him off the hook just because he had nice eyes and a sexy voice.

"I think I should formally introduce myself. I'm Ryker Jenson. I first met you online as Oblivion. Over the course of that year, we became friends. There was a lot of flirting, and I thought things might change once you turned eighteen, but then I never heard from you before our last mission."

Fury rose up in me, and I was thankful to have the two men beside me, or I might've stood up and thrown my perfect coffee in his face, and it was too good to waste it that way. Rolling my eyes instead, I scoffed before taking a sip of my healing liquid.

"Have something to add?" he asked, almost like he was amused.

"That's rich coming from you."

"It seems we're back at the impasse of yesterday, little hacker. Care to explain what grievances I've caused?" he asked, calm and collected. He had the nerve to smile at me, daring me to fight him.

"First of all, you were the one who never showed up that night. I was there, and Obsidian was on comms with me until the police showed up. I was arrested and charged with breaking and entering. I got off with community service only because of my parent's connections. My whole future was almost washed down the drain that night because you set me up to take the fall. Don't even get me started on Mongoose."

Ryker's face hardened, and he moved closer, making my whole body tense. "Finley, that's not what happened. Dex was with me on comms, so I'm not sure how he could've been in two places unless he was lying to one of us. I waited for you, but I went ahead when you were thirty minutes late."

"Likely story. I'm not falling for it. I know what happened. I have the mug shot to prove it."

Ryker held his hands up, approaching me like a scared animal and pissing me off even more. I wasn't the one remembering things incorrectly.

"I'm not saying you're wrong. I believe that you were arrested. I just think there's a flaw in both of our stories. Where did you go that night? Let's start there."

"The high school. I was told to steal the budget for that school year."

Ryker tilted his head, observing me. "And who sent you that information?"

"You did." He shook his head, my hackles rising again at his dismissal.

"No, I'm not saying you're wrong. I'm saying it wasn't me. Did you happen to crack the code I sent you the other day? It was access to a drive with all our conversations on it. I thought I was showing you our history, but it seems it might be even more important than I realized."

I looked up at Cohen, who was shuffling his feet, scratching the back of his head. "Did you?" I asked. Observing him, I was certain he knew something.

"Um, yeah. Sorry, with everything that happened yesterday, I forgot to mention it. There are conversations, like he said. Here, I'll grab them."

"It doesn't prove anything. You could've deleted things."

"You're right, but I didn't. But I can show you what I received from MKG on our last mission."

Huffing, I sat back, still cradling my mug. Taking another sip, it was more to have something to do while we waited. Asa put his arm around my shoulders, pulling me into his chest. Milo didn't overtly touch me, but his body pressed into mine, offering me comfort on both sides. Ryker's jaw tensed as he watched Asa and me, making me smile a little.

Cohen walked out with his laptop and sat on the coffee table. Once the server was open, he turned it around and handed me his computer. Ryker moved around the back of the couch, making me nervous now that I couldn't see him. He leaned over my shoulder, pointing to a folder.

"You can look at all of them later. I'm not hiding

anything, but check this one first so we can clear this up between us."

I clicked on the folder, heaviness filling my chest. Seeing the server messages had my hand shaking as I clicked on them. A thousand memories and emotions slammed into me, things I'd long since forgotten, things I hadn't wanted to necessarily remember. I closed my eyes, breathing deeply as I tried to calm my heart. Panic was edging around the corners of my mind, threatening to send me spiraling again.

"Breathe with me, Fin. Remember how we did it before? Breathe in your favorite color and let it fill you up, taking over all the corners of your fear. Now, slowly release all that fear, exhaling a color you hate. Let it go, exiting you. Again, in. Now, hold it, and release."

I did it a few times, feeling my three guys around me. I listened to Milo's voice, his smooth timbre making me feel calm. I exhaled and opened my eyes, turning to look at him. Nodding my thanks, I focused back on the screen, trying to read the messages.

MKG admin: Your team's final mission is to obtain a file on the blueprints for the new city building. All members must participate to pass. You have until midnight.

But… no. That didn't make sense. I blinked, but the information didn't change. So, how could we both be right? We couldn't. And Ryker's looked legit. Which meant… mine had been a ruse. But why?

"You're certain the message came from me?" he asked, not moving from behind me. I turned slightly, forgetting he was close, and almost bumped into him.

"Yeah. I, um, saved them." I escaped his gaze, focusing on Cohen. "May I?" I asked, pointing to the laptop.

"Of course, sweetheart. I told you I have no more secrets." Blowing him a kiss, I typed the address to one of my secure servers. My fingers hesitated over the keys as I debated opening this can of worms. Ryker sighed, thinking I didn't want to share my password, and moved back.

"I can't see anything," he muttered, sounding put out. For some reason, that brought me joy and gave me the boost I needed to open up this scab and hopefully heal this wound once and for all. With a deep breath, I typed in the password and clicked on the folder.

"Here," I said, opening the conversation from that last night.

Obsidian: Thirty minutes to go. Anyone need a reminder of the plan?

Blackhawk: Nope. You watch our backs, and Oblivion and I do the badass stuff.

Oblivion: Oh? I like being badass. Where are we going? And you're here?

Blackhawk: Secrets, little hacker. I couldn't miss out on meeting you.

Oblivion: So, where are we meeting?

Obsidian: Are you ever not flirting? I'll be on comms guiding you through. I have some things to do. I'll catch you guys later. Tonight we become official Knights!

Oblivion: Wahoo! Talk to you later.

Blackhawk: Later, Sid.

Blackhawk: Are you familiar with Clark Pleasant High School?

Oblivion: You're kidding, right?

Blackhawk: I'll take that as a yes. Meet me there at 10pm. We have a small window to get in and out before it's due. Are you ready, little hacker?

Oblivion: Definitely. See you there. And thanks for the gift.

Oblivion: Sorry, I know I'm not supposed to mention it.

Blackhawk: Yeah, no problem. See you soon,

little hacker.

"What the crap is this?" Ryker asked, looking at me like I'd grown a second head.

"The conversation we had." I stared at him, wondering how he'd become the head of a secret order if he couldn't decipher that.

"Yeah, I see that, except it never happened." He looked up at me, sincerity and truth ringing in his eyes.

"What do you mean?" Cohen asked. "If you didn't do it, then who?"

He gulped, looking back at the screen before he met my eyes. "Obsidian. He's the only one who was at both of our sites. He has to be the one that led us astray."

"But why? I thought Sid was my friend. Why would he want me to get arrested? He almost ruined my life."

My body deflated, and I sank into the couch. Ryker moved around to the front, handing Cohen his computer. He appeared nervous for the first time, wringing his hands as he debated something.

"I think I might know why. And if so, then you were right, Fin. It was my fault, and I'm so sorry for that."

Son of a biscuit eater. What now?

Three

FINLEY

RYKER STARED AT ME, remorse and regret heavy on his features. None of the cockiness I'd witnessed before present, and if anything, he looked ashamed of what he was about to tell me. It was something I was all too familiar with, and it made me soften toward him.

Taking a deep breath, I let it out slowly, preparing my battle armor for whatever he had to unburden. When he saw I was ready, he came around and sat on the coffee table, bringing him much closer than he had been.

"I'd really fallen for you over that year. I kept telling myself you were too young, but my heart didn't care. On that last mission, I was looking forward to meeting you and putting a face to the person I'd been crushing on. So, when I got word you weren't showing, I was crushed. I'd had this whole thing planned where I'd ask you out for your birthday. I wanted to get you some shoes you'd like so you'd have them to always wear."

"You did give me some shoes. You sent them to me and told me to wear them to the last mission. "

"No." Ryker shook his head, his eyes wide as he stared at me. "I never got up the courage to purchase any. I could never decide between the black or red ones."

"I distinctively remember you sent me red ones. Unless…" I looked at him, swallowing. My hands felt clammy as I wiped them on my legs. "You don't think he did, do you? How long had he planned to sabotage me then?" Anxiety was heavy as it swirled in my gut and I wanted to scream and run far away from this conversation.

"I'm starting to wonder if I even knew Dex." Ryker dropped his head, running his palms over his face. I glanced at Cohen who was staring at his handler with mixed emotions. "I feel like an idiot. All this time, I've been thinking of you and wondering why you never reached out."

"You thought of me?" I asked, dipping my head a little. For some reason, it was too personal to take head-on after the other news.

"More than I should. It's partially why the

remainder of that night is but a vague memory. I completed the mission, though barely, on my own. Not something I let Dex know. I had too much pride back then. When I returned to our room, he had shots ready. We toasted to a job well done and our invitation into MKG. Too many shots later and the heartache of losing you led to some poor decisions on my part." He sighed, scrubbing his hands down his pant legs, not making eye contact.

"What happened?" Asa asked when no one else spoke up.

"Dex made a move, and I didn't stop it. I was too drunk to care, and spending it being reckless felt like the right call at the time. Things went further than I'd intended, and I told him it was a mistake when we woke up the next morning. Something changed in him after that and the next year he transferred. We'd grown up together and had been on a few teams since we worked well with one another, but I hadn't ever considered him more than just a friend. But I guess..." He shrugged, his whole body deflating.

"Imagine that. You changing your mind in the morning," Cohen spat out before storming out of the room and slamming the door. I jumped at the noise, looking at the room he'd gone into, hoping he'd return. When he didn't, I turned my fury onto Ryker.

"Explain that!" I pointed, not letting him off the hook.

"Shit. Maybe I am a horrible person who deserves what is happening to him. I suck at relationships, okay? After things with you—"

"Nope, you don't get to use me as an excuse. Especially since it wasn't even my fault," I said, sitting up to fight him if I had to. Knowing the hurt Cohen felt made me want to go to battle for him. Shit, I think I *was* in love with the turd muffin. But what a hot muffin he was.

Thankfully, my weird thoughts gave me enough time to cool down and give Ryker a chance to talk before I kicked him in the groin again.

"You're right. I was hurt, but it didn't mean I couldn't have reached out or tried to talk to you. I let my past dictate how I felt and washed my hands of you, grouping you in with everyone else in my life that had left me. Needless to say, I have abandonment issues, or so my therapist tells me." He rolled his eyes, sighing. "Cohen and I met during training. We instantly became friends and worked well together. We teamed up on a few projects and had good success. After a tough case, I kissed him. I'd only meant for it to be a one-night thing. I'm embarrassed to admit I'd already been through most of the recruitment class that year. But it wasn't like the others, and that scared me. It lasted a little longer than most of my flings, but when I saw that he cared for me, I freaked out and ended our agreement. We've never been the same since. He left for a while, and I tried to forget him the same way I did you—working harder than anyone and only having one-night stands."

His phone pinged, and he pulled it out, sending a quick message before turning his attention back to me. It was apparent he was avoiding noticing the two guys next to me. I didn't know what his play was, but if it was to separate me from them, he had another thing coming. I wasn't even sure I liked him. He was attractive, but there was too much history for me to let him into my heart too soon.

Even though I knew that to be true, a small part of me whispered I wanted to. I shoved that thought away, knowing I couldn't entertain it at the moment. Cohen was hurting. I was hurting. That had to be remedied first and foremost.

"Sorry, I just pushed back a meeting. Where was I?" he asked.

"Something about your work ethic," Milo stated, twisting the last two words to the point they sounded rotten.

"Right." Ryker briefly looked over at him before returning back to me. "Avoiding my feelings led me to advance faster than anyone planned, and when the position became open, I stepped into the leadership role. I kept my post as Cohen's handler because it was a way for me to stay in his life at a safe distance. The anonymity within the organization allows me to live free among my peers without them knowing I'm their boss. Only a handful even know my real title."

"So how do I and MKG fit into all this?"

"The Order had recruited me like most of their initiatives when I was younger. That's how I knew Chaos and connected you. I didn't know he was Cohen until later when we met for training. After I made it into MKG, I worked with The Order to determine their end goal. Why was this group recruiting teens and young adults to steal information about schools, homeless shelters, and politicians? Why were they focusing on kids as their go-to members?"

I'd never thought about it that way. I hadn't thought about what their motive was for wanting me. At the time, it just felt like the answer I needed to get what I wanted.

"What did you find?" I asked, clearing my throat. Asa brushed his thumb against my hand, soothing me more.

"I don't have enough time to get into that now, but I was able to shut it down. I never told Dex that I was responsible. I graduated college a year later, and

I came here for training. Things had been weird with us since that night, and I didn't do anything to make them better. We talked off and on, kept up to date with one another, and occasionally would get together for a meal when one of us was visiting. As far as he knew, I worked at a security firm in Colorado. I never would've imagined he could've done all of this. He wasn't very assertive and would often wilt under pressure. It doesn't fit with the man I know."

"If it's not him, then we're back to it being you. So, what's it going to be?" I asked, crossing my arms. I narrowed my eyes at him, letting him know to not even entertain the idea it was me. There was no world where I would volunteer to get myself arrested.

He smirked, holding up his hands in defense. "I know, I know. The Occam's razor principle—the simplest answer is probably the correct one. If it's not you and it isn't me, then it has to be Obsidian, aka Dex. It's the only other explanation unless we're entertaining the theory a ghost planned it all?"

I furrowed my brow, taking lessons from Rhett. Ryker chuckled, the sound deep, making me want to roll around in it. Ugh, stupid sexy man with his sexy deep voice.

"So, how do we get ahold of Dex?" Cohen asked

from the side where he'd emerged, leaning in the doorway.

"I've been trying to since you mentioned it yesterday. He's not answering."

"And what does he have to do with MKG being back?"

"I'm not sure that he does. Right now, I'm not jumping to conclusions until we have all the facts. First, I'll talk to Dex and figure out why he would pretend to be me and send you to the wrong location. In the meantime, we focus on MKG as a separate entity. I was being honest when I invited you to join our ranks. We could use someone of your skill set. There's a training class that starts today. If you're interested, then Cohen can show you where to be."

"And if we're not?" I asked, trying to hide the thrill that had run through me at the prospect.

"Then we go our separate ways. I'll have to brainwash you so you forget our location and everything."

"Fuck that!" Asa shouted as Milo joined in with, "No way!"

"Funny," I deadpanned once the boys had quieted. "Be serious, Ryker."

A grin spread across his face, and he leaned forward a little, enough to bring the intoxicating scent of his closer to me.

"I like hearing you say my name, little hacker." He licked his lips, his eyes dilating a little.

Huffing, I crossed my legs, trying to ignore the throbbing between them. "Yeah, I'll remember that then. Answer the question before one of my boyfriends loses it on you, and your team has to rush in here again because your monitor shows you peed your pants." I smirked, his eyes narrowing at the use of boyfriends, plural.

"Then we'll discuss this on neutral grounds. Until then, you have a decision to make. I hope to see you at dinner. I'll have a private one set up for us."

He stood, his phone clutched back in his hand as he began to walk to the door, already typing on it.

"You owe Cohen an explanation too. Not just me."

He tensed, stopping briefly as his step stuttered before continuing to the door. I didn't think he would respond, but he turned, meeting my eyes and then Cohen's briefly, saying, "Fine," and then was out the door. The sound of it latching and then beeping as it relocked was the only thing we could hear for a solid thirty seconds until someone moved.

"Boyfriends?" Milo asked, looking at me sheepishly.

"Oh, um, yeah, sorry, I kind of lumped you into

that. I'm um, well." My face heated, and I realized the pile of dog poo I'd just stepped into.

"How about Cohen and I get some laundry started and check out the gym for a bit?" Asa said, getting up from the couch as he pulled Cohen with him, barely remembering to pick up the basket we'd dropped yesterday before they left.

The quiet filled the air, and I forced myself to turn and look at Milo. He was watching me and thankfully didn't look upset.

"So, um…" I mumbled, not knowing where to start.

"I'd love to be your boyfriend, Fin. I think we should get to know one another better, though. I know you have something with Cohen and Asa, and I'm still trying to figure out my place in your life. I like you and think we'd be good together, so maybe we just start there?"

"I think I can get on board with that. So, we're kind of dating?"

"Sure." He smiled, moving his hand to cup my face. "As much as we can in an underground secret bunker."

"Oh, I imagine we can be creative. But first, how about we just start off with a kiss?" My question came out hesitant, not sure how he'd respond. When he smiled, it felt like my heart might beat out of my chest as it raced to catch up with what was happening.

Milo leaned forward, his hand gripping my face firmer as he neared my lips. I watched every movement, cataloging them so I could remember this later. The feel of his hands, soft against my skin. The stubble on his jaw. How his eyes shimmered in the light. How it looked like he held his breath as he moved closer. But my favorite was how his eyelashes fluttered closed at the last second behind his glasses as his lips met mine.

It was tender and sweet and everything I knew Milo to be.

Tentatively, I raised my hand, placing it at the back of his neck, feeling the coarse hairs as I laid it there. When I didn't pull away, he moved his lips, pressing in harder. I gave him what he wanted, meeting his movements with my own.

When he pulled away, a whimper left me, my cheeks flaming, but I didn't feel too embarrassed by the pleased smile that spread across Milo's face.

"I look forward to courting you, darling."

Someone call the swoon police because I about melted.

Four

COHEN

I ONLY MADE it a few feet out of the laundry room before Asa opened his mouth, not letting me get away with anything. He'd been eyeing me the whole time while we sorted clothes, so I knew it was coming. I was just hoping I could outrun him and he'd forget. Didn't look like it was going to happen though.

"Sooo… how are you doing?" Asa observed me, his gaze earnest as he checked me over for any cracks in my foundation.

Blowing out a breath, I shoved my hands in my pockets as I kept walking. "Can we wait until we're not in the hallway?" I asked, deflecting.

"Sure, man."

I kept walking, leading him to the gym. We walked in, finding it empty for the moment. Asa spun around, taking it all in. It was a state-of-the-art gymnasium with every piece of workout equipment you could ever need, a boxing ring, a track that ran above the place, a shooting range, and several rooms for massages, ice tubs, saunas, and even a pool. Just about every sport was covered outside of the ice ones.

"Wow, this place is massive. I thought the hockey training rooms were cutting edge, but this is… I have no words."

"Yeah, it's pretty awesome." I smiled, enjoying his excitement. Of course, the gym brought with it a whole slew of emotions. Memories of my own training, sparring with Ryker, and my budding feelings for him plagued me, and I suddenly wondered if this was the best place to be at the moment.

"You okay?"

A sardonic laugh left me before I could stop it. "I don't think I can answer that."

"Okay, how about you start with how you feel about seeing Ryker." Asa walked over to the wall and slid down onto the mat. Sighing, I knew I could benefit from talking about my feelings, so I followed and joined him on the ground.

"I don't know where to start," I admitted, laying my head back against the wall. "When things ended with Ryker, I took some time away from The Order.

When I returned, I was anxious about running into him, but after a few months, when that didn't happen, I felt relieved and sad. It hit home that I'd just been a fling for him, so I moved on. But now, to learn that he's been my handler this whole time in secret is confusing. Did he do it to mess with me? Or did he care, and it was his way of staying in my life? My brain is going around and around, and I can't seem to land anywhere."

"I think that's one of those things you might have to ask him yourself. You'll never know the real answer otherwise."

I snorted, shaking my head. "If only it was that easy to talk to Ryker. He's not one for communicating."

"I dunno. I think you're remembering the younger version of him. While he might have some areas with Fin and you to make up for, I took him as a mature and serious leader. He might surprise you that he's changed since your last liaison."

"Maybe," I sighed. "But does that erase everything? I'm not sure I want to open my heart to him."

"A conversation is just that, a conversation. It's not a requirement to trust someone or forgive. It's just a chance to clear the air. I think you owe yourself that much. What you do from there is up to you."

"Yeah, I suppose you're right. Not to change the

subject, but what do you think about Milo?" I laughed, tilting my head slightly toward him.

He grinned, shaking his head. "I'm cool with it. Much like you, Milo has been hanging around for a while now, so I've kind of come to terms with it. Plus, he seems to bring something out in her neither of us does, and I like seeing that side of Fin."

"You're a lot more easygoing about this than I thought you'd be."

"I've thought about that myself, and as far as I can tell, I think being separated from my twin at birth broke something in me. My whole life, I've been searching for something to fit that space. I tried with my parents and only got pushed away by my father. I tried hockey, and it worked for a while. The team aspect was nice, and I instantly had a group of friends. It wasn't until I met Fin, Sawyer, and all the guys in her life that I finally felt like I belonged. I get that with you and Milo too. When we all worked together in the hotel the other day, it clicked for me. Together, we're all better with Fin, and I love that feeling."

I nodded, thinking it over. "Yeah, I think I know what you mean. The Order was that for me for a while, that place to belong. The fallout with Ryker had me feeling on the outside again. Working with Fin and Samson has been that home I think I was looking for. This past week has been the most natural my life has felt in ages."

"Which brings me back to the original topic… does Ryker fit into that? For you? For Fin?"

Taking a deep breath, I looked around the gym, hoping the answer would come to me. When it didn't, my shoulders slumped, and I turned back to Asa. "I don't know, and I can't answer that for Fin. If she wants him, then that's something I guess I'll have to figure out separately."

"So, for now, should we go through this training program?"

I smiled, some glee at what awaited them filling me. "I don't think it would be a bad thing. It would give Fin and us some time to work through things in this jumbled mess of secrets and lies. Besides, it's two weeks, still plenty of time to return to school in the fall if you plan to."

"Do you think we've given them enough time to talk about their feelings?" Asa asked, standing.

"As much as I'm willing to give," I admitted, standing up. "He can't have all of her time."

Laughing, Asa slapped me on the back, and we headed back to the room. As we drew near our door, Ryker rushed around the corner from the opposite direction. His face was slack, devoid of emotions, but I saw it in his eyes.

"What is it? What happened?"

He stopped in his tracks, looking between the two of us. If I didn't know better, I could've sworn he was gauging whether we were together.

"I need to know what you decided first."

"We were just about to go find out," Asa replied, walking up to the door and looking over his shoulder at me. Nodding, I followed him, and he placed his palm on the scanner and it beeped to let us in. He poked his head around, probably to give them time, so we weren't walking in on anything indecent since we had Ryker with us.

"Ryker has some news but needs your decision first," he said, stepping in. I followed, finding the two of them on the couch. Their lips were puffy, but they looked like they'd been talking otherwise.

"What do you guys want to do?" Fin asked, checking with us.

"I'm okay with it. Milo?" Asa answered.

"It's not how I imagined spending my time, but I'm game."

"Cohen?" Finley asked me.

My eyes heated as I met hers. "As much as I appreciate your concern, sweetheart, I'm afraid I'll be one of your trainers, not an initiate."

"Oh," she said. I could've sworn her cheeks heated, and her pupils dilated, but it was quick and gone when she turned toward Ryker. She took some time assessing him and finally let out a long breath.

"I'm not sure where I stand with you or The Order, but I guess the training program would give us time to figure that out. It looks like we're all in. So, what's this news you have to tell us?"

Ryker seemed to relax at her statement, moving closer to the couch. When he looked like he was going to sit next to her, I jumped over the back of it, falling into the seat. Asa snickered into his hand, taking the chair on the opposite side.

"I guess that seat is taken," Ryker said, giving me a teasing look I didn't want to acknowledge. Narrowing my eyes, I crossed my arms, but Fin pulled them apart, taking my hand. Smugly, I linked our fingers together, lifting my eyebrows now at Ryker as he sat on the coffee table. It was still too close for my comfort, but at least it wasn't right next to her.

"Did you hear back from Dex?" Fin asked when Ryker didn't immediately start talking.

"I think so. Cohen, I wanted you to hear this from me first because I knew you were close. Kristina was taken hostage on a mission last night, and I fear she didn't survive."

Gulping, I sat back, the news surprising me. "What happened?"

"Her team went to reconnaissance a building when they were ambushed. It's too early to tell, but the intel might have been false, luring them there for this purpose. She was taken after her team was tranquilized. When they woke up, all their gear and vehicles had been tampered with. It took them four hours to walk back to the safe house. They called in an hour ago to report it."

I realized then it was the messages he'd received while meeting with us. It made me respect his role and how difficult it must be to balance it all.

"What are the next steps? Why tell us?" Fin asked, proving she was perfect for The Order.

Ryker turned to her, and I realized we'd been having a silent conversation when his eyes left mine. "I'm telling you because I believe she was taken by MKG. And based on the package that showed up soon after the team reported in, I'd put good money on the fact that Dex is behind it."

He pulled out his phone and clicked on something, pausing briefly before turning it. "What I'm about to show you isn't pretty. Are you sure you want to see it?"

"Yes, I think I need to," Fin replied, squeezing mine and Milo's hands. Ryker nodded, letting her decide her limits, and turned the phone.

At first, I wasn't sure what I was seeing was real.

Lining the box were photos of Fin dressed in a red cocktail dress and red stilettos. She was younger, probably around the age I'd first met her. That was when it clicked that this must've been the night she was arrested. From every angle, there was a picture of her, and they pieced together in the box to highlight her face with a red circle around it like it was a sniper scope.

Finley gasped, her hands moving to her mouth as she took it in. I placed my arm around her, pulling her to me, hoping I was giving her some strength.

"That was the night I was sent to the wrong place."

Ryker's face softened at her words, something in him easing. "I'm glad to hear you believe me. Yes, I think this confirms that Dex was also behind that night. I'm not sure what his motive was. If he just wanted you off the team, there were easier ways to do it. Why did he deceive us both?"

"Because he's obsessed with you," Asa said, his eyes falling to us. He'd been sitting back with his hands steepled as he thought. When he noticed we were all looking at him, he leaned forward.

"You said he was a brilliant coder? Correct?"

Ryker nodded, focusing on Asa.

"You were roommates. He had access to your computer and phone and could hack any of your passwords. I've learned how easy it is to clone those things with the right access this past year. You'd never question it because he was your friend. I bet if we look back through some of the messages, there were more conversations neither of you had with the other. When did you start liking Oblivion where he would've noticed?"

Ryker thought about it, glancing at Fin before turning back. "Maybe after our third mission. It was probably about three months into it."

"It wasn't too long after that you found out I was a girl," she said, her voice quiet.

"So, you're saying that, he's what? Obsessed with me? So he went after Fin to keep us apart? That's ludicrous. We were only friends."

"To you, but he obviously wanted more," I spat, some of my anger coming out in my words.

Ryker hung his head, taking a few breaths. "I screwed up with you, Cohen, and I'm sorry for that. I got scared. I promise, though, it wasn't like that with Dex. It was a drunken mistake. You... you never were."

He held my eyes, sincerity shining through, but I didn't know if I could trust it. Turning my head, I tapped my fingers on my knee as I tried to figure out the piece we were missing.

"Why now?" I asked, interrupting whatever they'd been talking about.

"Pardon?" Ryker asked, giving me his full attention.

"Why is he just coming after Fin now? She's been living her life for six years without a peep from either of you. So, why now?"

"I don't know," Ryker said, leaning back to think. "I managed to assist The Order in shutting MKG down years ago, and the original people behind it are in jail. I even checked again today that they were still behind bars. From what I can gather, Dex has been quietly operating MKG from the dark web. It wasn't until the past month they even popped back up on The Order's radar. I didn't think it was too serious since they'd been gone for so long. When Fin initially messaged me on the old server, I worried it was connected, but after a few traces, I knew she was clean. I thought," he paused, clearing his throat. He sat up, reaching out a hand to Fin.

She peered at it, not sure what to do. Hesitantly, she placed her hand in his. I wanted to yank it away, but I wouldn't do that to her.

"I thought at first you were back to apologize for what happened. When you didn't say anything, I figured the best way to engage after so long was to play our game. I wanted you to join our ranks, but I needed to know for certain you were ready. So, I devised the tests."

She pulled her hand back. Her eyes narrowed as some of her sass rose to the surface. "By covering me in drinks, ruining my computer, and then dousing me in paint? Or was it the attempted drugging and abduction? Some game." She scoffed, rolling her eyes.

"That wasn't me. I saw the person follow you, and I intervened. I was fighting them off. I would never drug you or take you against your will, Fin."

She sat back, and I pulled her in tighter, happy to have her close to me. Ryker's jaw tightened at the embrace, and I smirked, unable to hide my enjoyment at his discomfort.

"It wasn't until then that I knew something else was at play."

"Do you think that was Dex?" Milo asked.

"Could've been, or one of his disciples from MKG sent on a mission. It was hard to gauge in that fun house."

"Speaking of, creepy place to meet," I said, unable to miss an opportunity to needle him some.

Ryker looked at me oddly. "I said the Ferris wheel, like in the book. But you sent back the funhouse."

"Fudge sauce!" Fin said, jumping up. "He

planned that. He's been manipulating our moves even now!" She began to tug at her hair as she paced the small space between the couch and table, stopping when she came to the legs of the three grown men. When she realized she had about two inches to pace, she fell into the couch, exasperated.

"I'm starting to believe you more," she admitted.

"We should thoroughly sweep our electronics and change any SIM cards just in case."

"I used burners the whole time. It has to be the server," Fin argued.

"You might be right. If he's head of MKG, he might have access to things on the dark web we hadn't considered. I need to meet with my team and debrief them on this new information. MKG is becoming slippery and more dangerous than we'd originally assessed."

"Will there be a team sent to retrieve Kristina?" I asked.

"As soon as we have a lead. I'll keep you apprised of it."

"Thank you. She was a friend. How are Ash and Caleb doing?"

"They're pretty shaken up. They're both in the infirmary if you wanted to visit."

Nodding, I gave him a grateful smile. "Thanks, I will."

Ryker stood, looking at the four of us. "Training starts in an hour. Good luck. I'll be in touch."

"Wait," Fin said as he made his way to the door. "Are we still having that meal together?"

Ryker's face lit up, and he nodded. "If you'd like to. I'd like the chance to talk without all this subterfuge hanging over us."

"I think that would be nice," she said, looking at me.

"Okay, I'll see you guys at dinner then."

He gave a half-wave before he opened the door, the sound of it latching close the only thing we heard for a few minutes as we all sat with our thoughts.

"So, what does one wear to training?" Fin asked, looking at me.

It was such a Fin question that it had me erupting in laughter, lightening the mood.

"Whatever you want, sweetheart. But maybe leave the stilettos for later?"

She slapped my chest, but I saw some of the fear from the picture lingering, and I vowed to do my damnedest to erase that from her.

We all changed clothes and headed to the gym, and for once, I looked forward to whipping some new initiates into shape.

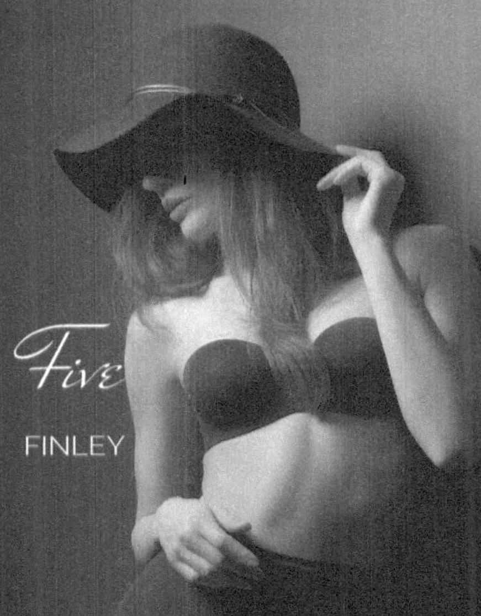

Five

FINLEY

STARING AROUND THE ROOM, I took in the other people present. It felt weird to call us initiates when I didn't even know if I wanted to do it. The group was a mixture of females and males—the females were outnumbered by only a few—in their early-to-late twenties. It was a diverse set of people, and something about that made me feel hopeful that I could belong somewhere.

Some of the group chatted as they stretched, while others stayed to themselves, eyeing everyone from the mats. The three of us were in the back dressed in athletic gear, Cohen giving nothing away on what to expect. He was up at the front with some of the other Order members. It was easier to pick out the trainers as they were dressed in all black and had a look about them like they were about to make us hurt and enjoy every second of it.

I glanced over to Asa as he touched his toes. "What do you think?"

"Not sure yet. Physically, I think we'll be okay. It's just if we have to do other tasks. Outside of you, I'm not sure what skills we have," he admitted, turning back to look at me sheepishly.

Leaning over, I kissed him, pushing some of his hair off his forehead. "Babe, you're amazing at everything. Don't underestimate yourself." He smiled, lighting my insides up.

"Well, I know first aid," Milo chimed in, making me chuckle.

"You know more as well." I turned to him, kissing his cheek. "I'm not worried about us working as a group. I'm curious if we'll have someone added and what this training entails since Co-bear wouldn't tell us anything," I huffed, crossing my arms as I stared at the man.

"Co-bear?" Asa laughed, slapping his leg. "Oh, I can't wait to tease him about that."

My cheeks flushed a little, but I shrugged. I wouldn't take it back.

"Alright, trainees. It's time to see what you're all made of. Line up."

Standing, I followed Asa with Milo behind me. I

didn't know if they did it on purpose, but they kept me in between them at all times. I liked it too much to say anything.

Cohen's eyes never left us as we headed to the front. I couldn't tell if he was nervous or excited from this distance, but the smirk that grew as we neared didn't bode well.

"Today, we'll gauge your physical limits," a man in his thirties with brown hair said as he assessed the line. "Eight laps equals a mile. Go."

Sighing, I started running with the group as they took off. Asa looked over at me, but I could tell he was holding back. "Don't wait on my behalf. Do your best."

He looked pained, but nodded, picking up his pace. Milo stayed with me, but at least it seemed like it was his natural speed.

"Running is the purest form of torture," I said after completing our first lap. Milo gave a hearty chuckle, but I didn't miss the fact that he didn't disagree. It looked like I'd have at least one partner in the non-workout camp. I much preferred only getting sweaty if naked bodies were involved.

I ignored the people around us, even when it seemed like others were lapping us. I didn't even look over at Cohen, too worried about what I'd see there. Was he disappointed I wasn't more of a kick ass girl? I could be kick butt in other ways, just not with running. It was the worst.

"One more," Milo panted, making me feel slightly better that my chest felt like it was on fire.

Nodding because I didn't have the breath to speak, I kept my eyes on the space in front of me. When we crossed the finish line, I collapsed to the ground, falling into a starfish. My face felt beet-red, and I had sweat in places sweat shouldn't be. My body tingled, and my muscles ached. I was beginning to reconsider the whole agreement to do this training if it meant doing *that* again.

A body stood over me, shielding the overhead lights. Looking up, I found a hand, so I reached up, taking it. Sighing, I sat up, realizing it had been Cohen. He handed me a water bottle, and I took it eagerly, barely remembering to drink it slowly, so I didn't make myself sick.

Once half of it was downed, I looked around, taking in the others. I was surprised when there were a few people still running. I hadn't tracked if we were last or not but had assumed we were. Everyone else was sitting around, talking as they stretched and drank water. Most looked as bright-eyed and fresh as they did when they started. I found Asa on my other side, noticing he fit in with that crowd.

"I kind of hate you," I said, taking a swig of my water. "You don't even look like you broke a sweat."

"Professional athlete, babe. It's kind of my job. I wouldn't be good at it if I couldn't run a mile."

"Ugh, you make it sound like that wasn't hard." I began to pout, falling back onto the floor. The guys laughed at me, Asa's head moving over mine.

"I'm not saying it isn't. Sorry, that came out insensitive. I just meant that I do this every day."

Before I could retort, the man who'd taken the lead began speaking again. "Not bad. You'll be running that every morning. Your speed should improve each day so that you've shaved minutes off your time by the end of the two weeks. Now, let's move over to the weights. I'm going to break you into two groups. One group will work on legs and the other arms. After thirty minutes, we'll switch. Stand when I call your name."

He looked down at a clipboard, and I prayed that I wouldn't be separated from Asa or Milo. He began to list names, and I breathed a little easier with each one when ours weren't called. "Michales, O'Connor, Green, Mitchell, Anderson, Guzman, Chang, Young, Lewis, and Sharp, you're with Bishop." They walked off toward a different section of the gymnasium before he looked down at the list. "The rest of you are with Cohen." He nodded toward my smirking boyfriend, and I prayed this wouldn't hurt too bad.

Who was I kidding? He'd make sure it did. I'd have to find a way to get back at him later. Thoughts of how I could punish him pushed me through the next hour as we rotated between arm and leg exercises. My body felt like jelly, but I was proud of myself for sticking it out. Asa still looked like he was one of the trainers, while Milo and I looked like the two people who'd be picked last for any group sport.

"That's it for physical today. Most of you did well. You get a few hours break before the night training. See your group leader for where to go. Dismissed." The leader, who I'd learned was Jack, walked off toward the locker room, a few of the other trainers following.

"I don't think I can move," I mumbled, attempting to pick up my arm.

Cohen chuckled before he bent over and picked me up into his arms. A few of the other recruits looked at our group as we exited, but I didn't care. Snuggling into Cohen's arms, I'd let him carry me wherever he wanted.

"Oh, is that so?"

Blinking, I realized I'd said that out loud, but I stood by it. "Yep." I smiled, my eyes already closing.

"Tell me that we have time for a nap before we have to meet Ryker?" I said around a yawn.

"You do, sweetheart. I'm just glad you're not mad at me."

"Oh, I am. I have plans of how to repay you for the torture. I'm just too tired at the moment. But it's coming."

I didn't hear his response as I gave in to sleep.

AFTER A NAP AND A SHOWER, I was feeling more like myself. My muscles still hurt, but they weren't as bad as I expected. Cohen was pouting, nervous about what torture I would give him, and offered to rub some cream into them later so that they wouldn't be killing me tomorrow. Looking at the contents of my suitcase, I was itching to make something new, but time didn't allow for it today. I'd have to see if there was access to a sewing machine at some point. I'd gone too long without touching one. I was having withdrawals.

Pulling out a nice pair of dark jeans, I matched it with a criss-cross top that tied in the back, leaving most of my back exposed, meaning no bra. I could get away with it since my boobs were small. Adding hoop earrings, black heels, and a drop necklace, I did one more turn in the mirror before taking in my look.

A whistle at the door had me peeking over my shoulder, finding Asa watching me. "You look amazing. I love how you can just pull an outfit together." He walked closer, his eyes heating up as he noticed the front. "Shit. Making it through this dinner just got harder. Pun intended." He smirked, wrapping his large hands around me.

Picking up my lipstick, I watched as Asa tracked every move I made as I finished off my look. I spread the bright red shine across my lips, feeling confident as I stared back at the person in the mirror. I hadn't really taken stock since arriving here, mostly because I'd passed out and then was hit with more information than I could process, but taking it in now, I realized that I did feel lighter.

I'd found Blackhawk and was getting answers for what happened that night.

It wasn't what I'd believed, but it was still making the things from my past right, which felt good. I no longer felt like a shadow was hovering over me, just waiting to swoop in and cover me the second I forgot to pretend I was happy.

And maybe that was the most considerable relief of all. I wasn't pretending.

Things with Asa were better, and I wasn't hiding

how I felt about Cohen and Milo anymore. I wasn't alone. In fact, I had people in my corner helping me fight the ghosts from my past. While I hadn't made the best decision to run off on my own, it had led me here, which was oddly where I needed to be.

Things were coming together, and I found that part of me I'd pushed aside, coming alive again. The Order could be a chance to explore that and figure out who I was becoming. I couldn't deny that I was changing. My life was moving in a new direction, and it felt right.

"You look amazing," Asa whispered, his breath hitting my cheek. He'd dropped his head down to my shoulder during my musings.

"Thanks. I feel amazing."

He smiled at me, still making my insides flip. A knock at the door broke our eye contact in the mirror as we turned to find Cohen. He took me in, his Adam's apple dipping as his eyes trailed down my frame.

"Damn, sweetheart. I think we need to skip dinner."

"That's what I said." Asa chuckled, dropping his arms from me. Reaching down, he took my hand and pulled me toward Cohen. "But I think you both need this dinner to clear the air. I wasn't sure about Ryker at first, but I think he deserves to be heard. And whether either of you is ready to admit it, you want to. I'm not saying you have to let him back into your hearts, but you might find he's a good friend."

I sighed, nodding. "You're right. And I think I'm ready. I'm not as mad as I was, and I can admit that I might have been putting all my shame and regret onto him instead of dealing with it myself. This adventure has at least made me face my own inadequacies as painful as it was."

Asa kissed my head. "I'm proud of you, Fin."

"Guess it's time I get over myself too," Cohen sighed. "Let's do this."

We walked out into the open area, finding Milo waiting. He had on the bowtie he'd worn the first day, and I smiled, loving seeing him in it. Asa nudged me forward, so I dropped his hand and walked to Milo.

"You look handsome," I said, just as he said, "You're beautiful."

We both blushed, and I took his hand, leading him to the door. There were some nerves in my belly, but I knew no matter what else was disclosed tonight, I was proud of myself for how far I'd come, and I had three men to help me wrestle through it.

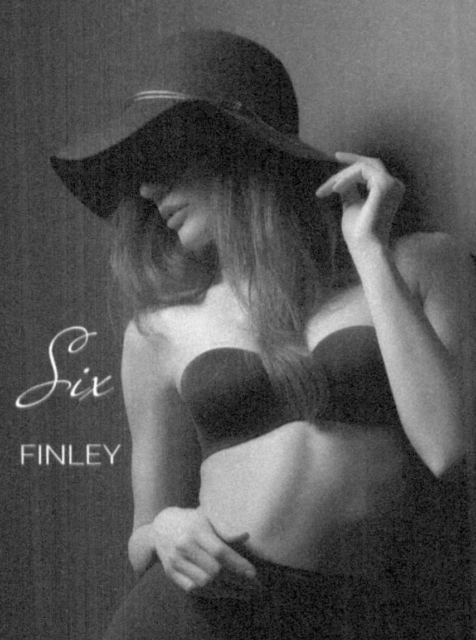

APPREHENSION WEIGHED on my shoulders as we took our seats around a huge table filled with food. Ryker wasn't here yet, making me even more nervous for some reason. A guard stood at the door, but other than him, the room was empty.

"Where do you think he is?" I asked, just as a door opened, revealing Ryker in a suit. I swallowed, not having expected to see him dressed up. It really was criminal the way he filled it out. He was dangerous in regular clothes, but in a tailored suit that fit him just right, he was downright lethal.

"No fear, little hacker, I'm here." His smug smile reminded me why I had to keep my guard up, so I let my mouth take over without thought.

"Not scared, just didn't want to waste this good food. Now that you're here, we can eat." I picked up my fork, shoved something into my mouth, and chewed. I smiled like it was the best thing I'd ever eaten, but in reality, I wasn't even sure what it was.

The guys shifted, attempting to hide smiles as Ryker only nodded, picking up his fork and taking a bite. When it became too quiet, and I wasn't even able to enjoy the food, I broke, assenting to the fact that he'd won this round.

"Fine. You win. Talk. That's why I'm here. How is MKG back, and why didn't you know Obsidian or Dex was running it if you've been talking all these years?"

Cohen choked on his bite as he tried to hide his smile at me giving in. I stuck my tongue out at him, promising retribution for later. Ryker took his time finishing his bite, setting his fork and knife down, and then wiping the corners of his mouth. It was a stall tactic, and it was doing exactly as he intended— driving me crazy.

A hand clamped down on my leg, squeezing, and I tried to steal some comfort from Asa. His thumb stroked back and forth, sending tiny ripples through me. Sucking in a breath, I forced myself to count to ten before I let it out and glanced back up at Ryker.

He was watching me with concern on his face, and the act dropped. "I'm sorry, little hacker. Sometimes, it's easy for me to fall back into that role without realizing it. You push all my buttons, making me want to push yours in return. You're right; we're here to talk. Let me start at the beginning and give you the full scope." Sighing, he took a long drink of his tea before placing the glass back on the table.

"After a year undercover, The Order was able to shut MKG down. It was run by a crime lord who'd discovered that if he used teenagers and young adults, he not only had access to things he typically wouldn't, but they were naive enough to follow orders without questioning them if they were getting paid. Everyone wants to belong at that age, and MKG gave people that. He filled their pockets and kept them happy, and they, in return, were willing to look the other way or not question the things they were doing."

I took another bite of my food, pondering what he was saying. It rang true. I'd been so desperate for information I hadn't stopped to ask why I needed to steal things. And because of that recklessness, someone had died. I didn't know what Mongoose's story was, but it still haunted me today, and I felt responsible.

"That makes sense. So, how did you shut them down?"

"I moved my way up the ranks and discovered who the man behind it was. Cruz Ayers and two of his cronies were put away. When I checked this morning, they were still in prison. I'm not sure when Dex revitalized MKG. That's something I'm curious about as well."

He took another bite of his food, and I took the opportunity to do so too. Chewing over his words, I tried to sort them in my head and what I wanted to know next. It felt like this was the one chance I would have to ask him whatever I wanted, and I didn't want to waste it.

"How did you become the leader here?" I asked, realizing that was what I wanted to know most. The past was important, but it didn't feel as vital for some reason. This was odd for me since the past led me here, but now that I was, it felt like I'd been able to move beyond it for once and look ahead to the future. A future that was still uncertain.

Ryker sat his fork down, and I realized he was finished. He sat back, his arms relaxing on the arms of the chair. My brain struggled with putting together the guy from the bar, the man in front of me, and the boy I'd talked to online for a year. He seemed like a million different versions of himself, and I wasn't sure which one was true. I wanted to believe I knew the real him, but with espionage being his job, it felt naive to do that.

"It wasn't something I sought out to take on. The

Order operates differently than most organizations. Our prime objective is to make sure no one becomes too powerful. 'We restore the balance.' But every organization needs a leader, or there will be chaos and it will collapse from within. So The Order created a shifting leadership position and kept it anonymous. It works to even the playing field amongst our agents, keeping allies and rivals out of our personal lives. I was approached two years ago to be the next leader. Each head of The Order serves two years unless in a crisis, then the board may elect to keep them on until things have calmed."

"So, your time is almost up? What happens then?"

He smiled, liking my question, and I couldn't understand why. "The board is a rotating selection of previous leaders. So, once I've served my two years, I'll make my recommendation for my replacement and then take my place on the board to serve as a mentor for the next leader."

"Does it work? Keeping corruption and power grabs from tainting The Order?" Milo asked. I turned, knowing he would be the best to understand the hierarchy of a secret organization being connected to the Council.

"It's the best I've seen try. There are other measures in place that I'm not at liberty to discuss, but over the years, The Order has kept their purpose of serving others and keeping the balance."

"How old are you?" I asked, instantly curious. "You never would tell me when we talked."

"That's because I felt like a huge perv falling for a seventeen-year-old girl." He sighed, shifting a little. I didn't focus on how his shirt tightened around his chest muscles. Nope. Not me.

"I'm 26, the same as Cohen."

I turned to Milo, instantly curious how old he was. He smirked at me, apparently knowing what I was about to ask.

"I'll be 26 in a few months."

"Hmm, I guess Asa and I are the babies at 22." I barely refrained from saying I apparently had a type for older guys. Strike that from your brain, Fin! I did not need to encourage Ryker. Three guys were enough to handle.

I looked up after scolding myself to find the table all observing me. I wiped my mouth, afraid I'd somehow smeared something when they all started to laugh. My cheeks heated when I realized they were just watching me. I wasn't used to this much male attention directed at me. It was weird.

"I know we still have a few things to discuss. How about we move to somewhere more comfortable? I think I'll need some drinks for the next part."

Ryker looked around, and I realized everyone else had finished eating. I quickly shoved the last few bites of food into my mouth, my cheeks pouching like a chipmunk as I nodded.

Cohen laughed, his shoulders shaking as he got up and walked over to me. "Sweetheart, you could've taken your time."

Shrugging my shoulders, I took his hand, wanting to ask how he was doing as we followed Ryker. Once I had the food swallowed, I bumped him, getting him to look down at me. I pointed to Ryker, lifting my eyes. He smiled, one corner of his mouth lifting with the gesture before he shrugged. I watched his face for a few seconds before nodding that I understood. It was complicated, but he was okay for the time being.

Same, dude, same.

When we stepped into a smaller space, I was instantly hit with Ryker's smell making me realize this had to be his space. It was so concentrated it made my skin break out in goosebumps, and I wanted to do a full-body shudder at the intoxicating scent. Cohen's nostrils flared next to me, and in some weird way, it made me feel better that I wasn't being tortured alone.

Ryker directed us to a seating area, and I took a seat, Cohen on my left and Milo on my right. Asa took one of the chairs positioned where he could see the door. He might not be trained as a spy, but I could see some of his time with his dad was paying off. He was a natural.

Ryker pointed to a drink cart as he began to fix himself something. Cohen stood and walked over, making some drinks for the rest of us. I watched them as they stood close to one another, trying to figure out their relationship. Ryker's hand brushed against Cohen's as he handed him the tongs for the ice, his eyes immediately jumping to the man in question. When Ryker didn't do anything, Cohen took them and finished his drinks. I had no clue what he'd made, but I took it, thanking him. He looked somewhat frazzled, and I wondered if *he* even knew what he'd made.

Ryker sat in the other spinning chair across from Asa, shifting to look at the three of us on the couch. "So, I've told you about The Order and how it works. What's next?"

"You didn't know Dex was behind it?" Milo asked, bringing up the question from earlier.

"No, we talk every now and then, but it's been a while since I've seen him in person. He kind of went underground after MKG shut down. Once I gradu-ated college, there wasn't anything that connected us. I realize now that might have been callous of me, but at the time, I was focused on The Order, and Dex wasn't part of it. We were friends of convenience, and outside that one time together, we didn't cross the line. That makes me a shitty friend, I suppose."

"I can understand things from your point of view," I said, twirling the glass around in my hand, too nervous to drink it. The condensation felt nice against my skin, helping to cool me. "But, it doesn't change the events that occurred. There are things we must own up to if we move forward."

"You blame yourself for Mongoose," Ryker said. I held his eyes, nodding. Tears began to fill in mine, but I didn't shy away from this. I had to own it. He deserved that much respect. "Mongoose wasn't your fault, Fin."

I wiped a tear, shaking my head. "He asked for help, and I left him on his own. I didn't tell him to go into that building, but I didn't tell him not to."

"Wait, is this about the Magnolia safe house?" Cohen asked, drawing my attention.

"Safe house? I thought it was a homeless shelter. How do you know about that?" I asked Cohen, but it was Ryker who answered.

"This was what I wanted to talk to you about. MKG had found a list of Order safe houses. Magnolia was one of them. Mongoose was being bullied by someone, and in an attempt to find out who they were, he almost ruined my cover. He got close to the truth, so The Order made him a deal. I didn't learn about this until years later. They faked his death and helped him create a whole new identity."

"So, he's not dead?" I asked, hope blooming in my chest.

"Well, I don't know for sure his current well-being. But he didn't die in a house fire five years ago."

I sat with that knowledge for a few seconds, letting it course through me. The rest of the tears I'd been holding fell, and I breathed a sigh of relief. Maybe I wasn't so bad at this after all?

"Now that I've told you about myself over the past few years, what have you been up to?"

Smiling, I gave him a brief synopsis of how after juvie and community service, I turned to white hacking, helping people who needed it. I went to fashion school, graduated early, and followed Henry to TAS to design costumes and be their social media manager.

"I met Asa last year, and we became friends. When Sariah, or Sawyer as she goes by now, showed up, things got a little crazy. Turns out, she's Asa's twin sister. I learned about the Council and was almost sold in a human trafficking auction, but Milo saved me from that. Cohen was helping me find a pervert, and he stayed around after. I worked with the Agency and then Samson's security company after it was disbanded. It's been a crazy year, but I've learned a lot and grown. It's why I knew I had to come and face you, or well, the person I thought was responsible for getting me arrested."

"Now that you know it wasn't me, what do you plan to do?"

I looked to the guys, not knowing how to answer this. "I guess it depends on them. We agreed to do the two-week training course, so I guess I'm here for the next two weeks."

"Then I guess I have two weeks to convince you to stay."

"Stay?" I shook my head. "I don't know about all that. But what do you plan to do about MKG?"

"If Dex is behind it, then we'll go after him. MKG is dangerous, and if they're still operating, then that's bad news for everyone. Starting tomorrow morning, I'd like you to join the task force I'm creating to take them down. Each of your unique skills will give us an edge."

"I can't speak for them, but I started this journey for that reason, so I'd like to see it to the end." The guys watched me, and I wasn't sure what they would say. Cohen was the first to answer.

"I'll join. My other assignment ended, so you

know I'm free." Ryker nodded, looking to Asa and Milo.

"If Fin's there, then so will I," Asa said like that was the answer to everything.

"Same," Milo said.

It filled me with an emotion I wasn't used to, and as my cheeks heated, I ducked my head, unsure if I liked it or if it was scary.

After chatting a little longer, we headed back to our room, I couldn't deny that Ryker wasn't the douchecanoe I thought he was. I didn't trust him entirely yet, but I was warming up to him more and more. That night as I lay in bed, I replayed everything that happened, looking for any sign of falsehood. After an hour, I had to admit I couldn't find any. It looked like Ryker was going to get a second chance. Knowing him, though, it wouldn't take long for him to muck it all up. A smile spread across my face, and I knew I was hoping he did. He was much easier to hate when he was in the doghouse.

Him and his stupid suits that smelled too good.

Seven

FINLEY

AFTER AN ABBREVIATED training session in the gym, we were directed to a conference room. We'd been given fifteen minutes to shower and change. This whole spy life was not meshing well with my need to primp and accessorize. They were out of their minds if they thought I could wash, dry, and style my hair in fifteen minutes. Suffice to say, I barely managed to wash off, deodorize myself, and dress in basic leggings and a shirt in that time frame.

Huffing, I slunk down into an empty chair, attempting to braid my damp hair. Everyone else looked put together, making me instantly jealous of them. I took a moment to look around as they focused on the person at the front. The guys were behind me, having saved me the chair, so I smiled my thanks as I surveyed the group.

When Ryker walked in, I sat up straighter, smoothing down my shirt until I realized I was doing it and forced my hands into my lap. None of that. I did not need to primp for Ryker. The room grew quieter as he strolled to the front, his gaze assessing everyone. I tried not to let it bother me when it slid over me without a second glance. He couldn't play favorites. I knew that. But it still stung.

Dropping my eyes, I fiddled with my hands as I sucked in a deep breath. I couldn't let it affect me. This was a professional agency, and I didn't need to allow my feelings to muddy it. Pressing my palms down on my pants, I looked up, ready to listen. I caught Ryker's gaze just before he glanced away, and the concern there had me reassessing things. Okay, I could do this.

"Welcome, recruits. I'll be going over combat strategy today and then separating you into teams. You'll each be given a handler and objective. Your purpose is to complete your objective. The team that finishes first will be awarded a night off while the other teams rotate night watch."

An excited murmur started up around the room. I watched my peers, trying to figure them out, but they all blended together. Though, that might be the point. If there was nothing that distinguished them from the crowd, they were easily forgotten and able to sneak in and do what was needed while keeping a low profile.

If there was one thing about me, I was the oxymoron of a low profile. The fact I'd worn a red dress and stilettos to steal something confirmed it. In the past, that might've bugged me, but at this point, I owned the fact I was my own person. Even if that meant I didn't have a career as a professional spy, I was okay with that. I'd just have to figure out my adrenaline problem another way.

When I focused on the room, I realized they were already listing off teams. For Ryker's sake, he'd better have placed me with my guys, or I'd glitter bomb him so hard he'd be picking it out of his teeth for weeks.

"… Team three is Michales, Hemp, Doe, Young, and Black. See Bishop for details. This leaves our last team to Reyes, Welch, Bellamy, Sharp, and Guzman. You're with Campbell. Now strategy time."

Ryker rolled up his sleeves, exposing his tanned forearms, his veins popping as he flexed the muscles, and I had to physically remind myself to not get caught staring. I mean, to not check him out. Ew, gross. A snicker behind me made me believe I hadn't been as covert as I intended.

Over the next hour, Ryker displayed his knowledge and skill in how to approach a hostile situation.

I'd managed to take notes, finding his pointers helpful. He had a natural flair for teaching, and I wondered if he'd ever considered another career path. He was only twenty-six. Surely this wasn't his end goal? Besides, he was about to retire, or whatever, and be a mentor. As much as people boasted about retiring early, I doubted anyone wanted to do that at twenty-six. I'd get bored so quickly; I'd be making outfits for everyone out of all the curtains and sending them off to sing as they skipped along.

Okay, so I might have a slight obsession with the *Sound of Music*, but it didn't make it any less true.

"Right, that covers what you'll be doing tonight. Any questions?"

A pretty brunette raised her hand, her eyes shining as she looked at Ryker, making me immediately want to stab her with my pen. Lying it flat, I sat back, hoping the homicidal urges would also lessen.

They did not.

Going to my happy place of no budget in Mood Fabrics as I perused the aisles to later being shouted at by Tim Gunn *"to make it work"* I almost missed it when the meeting was dismissed.

You're so right, Tim Gunn. I just need to make this work. I have this in the bag.

Scooting back in my chair, I found my three guys looking at me with a mixture of odd expressions on their faces. "What?" I asked, wiping my face in case I'd drooled from the no budget dream. I narrowed my eyes as I tried to figure out what had them looking at me that way.

"You were whispering to yourself," Milo said, taking pity on me. "Something about 'making it work,' and you wouldn't let Tim down?" He said it with a slight question in his voice, almost as if he wasn't sure if that was correct or not.

Asa laughed, placing his arm around me as we began to leave the conference room. "Tim Gunn is Fin's spirit guide. Whenever she's stressed, she watches him on repeat."

"How do you know that?" I asked, my cheeks tinging red at being called out.

"We've been dating for almost a year. I've caught you with it on when I've been over. I might not know the difference between Valentino and Tom Ford, but I know Project Runway is your safety blanket."

Sighing, I smiled, squeezing his hand that was draped over me. "Yeah, something about Tim Gunn yelling at other people really settles me."

Cohen and Milo laughed, but it was more in spirit and not at my expense, making me relax more. We followed who I suspected were the other two members of our team to a private room down the hallway. I glanced at the girl and guy who joined us, but like before, outside of noticing they were fit and attractive, my brain couldn't latch on to any details about them. In fact, once Cohen began talking, I forgot all about them.

"Alright, Team Campbell, I'll be your handler during this mission. My role is to supervise only. I won't step in unless someone is in danger. This is a real mission and should be treated as such. If you can't handle this, then you're not Order material."

Everyone nodded, and I crossed my legs, liking Cohen's take-charge voice a little too much if the zing in my lower regions was any indicator. He smirked at me briefly, catching my shifting, only flooding my panties a little more.

"Tim Gunn, Tim Gunn, Tim Gunn," I chanted, making sure it was only in my head this time.

Cohen flicked on a screen, and our objective popped up. "This is a bakery that one of our sources states has a very eclectic clientele. Rough men and women come and go with pink boxes of cupcakes and pastries at all hours. Every day, like clockwork."

"You think it's a money-laundering scheme?" I asked, my brain already connecting the dots and the weak areas to exploit.

"Yes. We believe the cakes are used to disguise the money coming and going from the bakery. From our surveillance, a separate ledger is written into when these pink boxes are collected. That's what you're after. Get the ledger and provide evidence. Your only rule is to not get caught. You can use any of your talents; otherwise, I'll leave you to discuss. I'll be back in thirty minutes and expect to hear your plan. If it doesn't sound feasible, you fail before you even begin."

Swallowing, I thought through all the pitfalls as Cohen left, my brain running a mile a minute. As the others began to brainstorm, I took out my notebook, reviewing the notes that Ryker had given us. Some memories from MKG also surfaced, and I pulled on those strings of nights we discussed our plan of attack.

"It's easy. We go in, we punch them out, and take the book," the neutral male said, making me roll my eyes.

"You really think a bakery frequented by bikers and the like will let you just walk in and punch them? Please," I sighed as I focused on the paper, flipping through the screen until it showed the blueprints. "There is a small window of time when they're closed. We'll strike then. Here are our entry points. We'll need someone to disable the cameras and the alarm and stand guard. Two people will then enter the building and retrieve the book. If we do it right, we'll be in and out in under two minutes." I finished drawing the plan and looked up.

The girl was watching me and assessing my gaze on her as she pondered it over. Her male counterpart seemed to have a few screws loose as he scoffed, kicking his legs up on the table like he was king.

"Let me guess, princess, you're one of the two? I saw you eye-fucking our leaders. If you think you can get into The Order through your pussy then you're sorely mistaken."

Asa sat up, ready to strike, and I felt Milo tense next to me. I placed an arm across Asa's chest, stopping him. But before I could even retort, the girl punched him in the junk. The mouth-breather crumpled to the ground and I decided I liked her.

"That was awesome. What's your name?"

"Nicole Sharp." She stuck out her hand, and I took it, shaking it.

"Finley Reyes. So, that makes that mouth-breather, Guzman?"

She nodded, casting her eyes down at him like he was scum, making me like her even more. "Yep. He thinks that because his big brother is in The Order, he's a shoo-in. The tool can't keep his mouth shut long enough to keep himself out of trouble."

Chuckling, the guys settled back now that the douche was on the floor whimpering. "I'd offer to get you some ice, but yeah, suffer those purple balls. Anyway, I guess that means he's out. What about the rest of us? What are our skills?"

After a few tweaks, we decided I would disable the cameras and security system. Milo and Nicole would go in to retrieve the book while Asa stood guard outside. Guzman was relegated to van duty with me to monitor things. When Cohen appeared a few minutes later, we explained our plan to him, and he nodded, seeming pleased.

"You didn't want to be the inside person?" he asked me.

Shaking my head, I looked him in the eyes when I answered. "No, I know my skills and would be best at manning the systems. Based on the preliminary surveillance, they shouldn't be too difficult." He watched me, almost like he expected me to start laughing and say I was only joking and I'd be the one running into danger. When I didn't, he nodded, looking at the rest of the group. Guzman was now sitting at the table, scowling with his arms crossed, and I bet they were protectively covering his man berries as well.

"Alright. Sounds like you've all thought of everything. You have two hours to eat and gather whatever you need. Meet on level 1 at 20:00. If you're late, it's a strike, and we leave without you."

Everyone nodded, gathering their things, and we headed out the door. Together as a unit, we walked to the cafeteria to grab some food, getting it to go. The guys were quiet as we walked back, and I wondered what they were thinking, but my mind was too focused on the task and the need to ensure this one succeeded.

Eight

ASA

FINLEY WAS EATING HER FOOD, but I didn't think she was tasting it. She was lost in her thoughts as she ran over the plan in her mind. I knew this was important to her. She felt like she'd let people down in the past and failed; this was her chance to redeem part of her soul. But it didn't mean she had to do it alone.

"Babe?" I asked, nudging her.

"Hmm?" She looked over, but her gaze was far away.

"I think you need to get out of your head before tonight."

"What do you have in mind?" Cohen asked, a smirk beginning to form on his face.

I glanced to Milo, who was watching her, and I wondered how much I could push this. They were still figuring out one another and weren't there in their relationship yet. But it felt like we needed to be a solid unit to succeed.

My sister's relationship suddenly made sense to me. Not that I ever wanted to think about my twin being with seven guys, most of whom were my friends and teammates, but she'd created a family unit. She had an unbreakable bond with each of them, giving her the strength she needed to go up against our father and the Council.

We needed to forge ourselves together so nothing could come between us, and it felt like I was the commander of this ship. It was going to be me who brought us all together.

Standing, I held out my hand to Fin. She didn't hesitate, taking it, making my heart swell at her absolute trust. Smiling, I pulled her into my arms, holding her close for a hug. Dropping my head, I whispered my plan into her ear.

"I think you should let us bring you pleasure. You need to quit worrying about all the things that could go wrong and relax. You coming a couple of times should do the trick."

She sucked in a breath, pulling back to look at me. I showed her the heat in my eyes and nudged her with my erection. Lifting her chin, I dipped my head for the last bit.

"I know you're not there with Milo, so let him watch. Think of this as a group bonding project. One where the goal is to give you multiple orgasms."

"Let's try not to kill me," she teased, her eyes dancing with delight. My words had done the trick, and she was no longer locked away in her head. She glanced over at Milo, licking her lips as she nodded. "Okay."

Cohen and Milo looked at us, unsure what was going on. Taking my command seriously, I turned to them both.

"Our first mission tonight is to make Finley forget and to relax. The best course of action for that is several orgasms. You both game?"

Cohen stood and was stripping his clothes in the next second. Milo hesitated, and I could see the no on his tongue. Fin didn't need that right now.

"Your role is to watch and learn, Milo." He glanced at me, some slight fear in his eyes, and I wondered if I'd read the room wrong. Was he not interested in her that way? Maybe he didn't want to be part of a group scene? Didn't Sawyer say they all had a boundaries talk? Shit. Perhaps I should have started there.

Before I could spiral too far, he nodded, standing as he took a deep breath. He didn't take his clothes off like Cohen had, but followed him into the room.

He tried to hide the bulge growing in his pants, making me feel marginally better about assuming things.

Picking Fin up, she giggled as I swung her in my arms, carrying her the rest of the way to the room. Even though this suite had two bedrooms, we'd all been bunking in the bigger one. It was another reason I'd assumed Milo would be okay with being with everyone. Cohen was already down to his boxers as he sprawled out on the bed, and I began to think about how I wanted this to happen. I was going to need to read some of those books like Soren so I could get some ideas on how all of this worked at this rate.

Tossing Fin on the bed, I grinned as she bounced, rolling into Cohen's legs. "Let me help you out of your clothes, sweetheart," he said, grabbing her.

While Cohen occupied Fin, I looked around the room, finding Milo nervously standing against the wall. Walking toward him, I tried to ease him from looking like a scared animal.

"If you're not ready for this, you don't have to stay. No one wants you to feel uncomfortable. I just didn't want you to feel left out. I probably should've asked you beforehand what you were comfortable with, but with everything going on, we haven't really had a chance to talk about it."

Milo looked at me, swallowing. "If you're all okay, then I'm okay. I just don't know what to do."

I shrugged one shoulder, glancing back at the two on the bed. "Whatever feels natural."

Tugging at the back of my shirt, I decided to take my own advice instead of working out logistics and go with what worked. Tossing the material to the ground, I slipped my shorts, boxers, and socks off as I walked the rest of the way to the bed. Fin and Cohen were kissing as she straddled him, parts of her clothing still on like they'd both gotten distracted midway through.

Running my hands up her back, I unclasped her bra and slid it off her shoulders. Moving down to her panties, I lifted her up a little as I moved them down one leg at a time. She adjusted with me but never broke her kiss, making me smile at their commitment and total loss of the world around them. Knowing that it was just as likely for me to do that, I turned to Milo as he settled into a chair.

"Set an alarm for thirty minutes before we need to be upstairs." He nodded, pulling out his phone, satisfying my concern, and I looked back to the two on the bed. Cupping her breasts in my hands, I fondled them between my fingers, tweaking her nipples.

Fin gasped, releasing her mouth from Cohen's as she peered back at me. "About these orgasms, you promised me." Her pupils were fully blown, lust driving her, which was beautiful to behold.

"I'm ready to deliver." Reaching into the drawer, I pulled out some condoms, tossing one to Cohen, who caught it in his hand. Fin looked at them, biting her lip.

"I was thinking…" she started before I cut her off with a kiss.

"Not today. We can talk about it later." She nodded, satisfied with the answer for now.

Rubbing my palms over her backside, I kissed her nape, nipping it as my tongue lavished her skin. Cohen's fingers were already pumping in her, and she writhed on them, bucking as she sought them out. I'd planned to start with oral, but at this rate, I didn't know if she'd last.

"More," she panted, and I glanced over, catching Cohen's eyes. At his nod, I slid on the condom with ease, my cock hard and waiting.

Nudging her ass checks with the head of my cock, I began to rock back and forth as I dragged it through her wet folds. Her moan was all the encouragement I needed as I pushed forward, slipping inside her. Her pussy fit around me like a glove, and I gripped her hips tight as I held back the need to slam into her.

"Fuck, Fin. You feel so good," I groaned. She

wiggled as she whimpered, and I knew I needed to move for both our sakes.

Focusing on the task at hand, I eased back slowly and then pushed in. I kept it at a slow pace, driving us both wild with need, refusing to push it too soon.

"Please," she whimpered, "I need more."

Her cries were too much, and I gave in to the desire running through me. I didn't even notice the other two in the room at this point. The only thing I was focused on was Fin, and how her amazing pussy gripped my dick perfectly. Slamming into her this time, she grunted, wiggling back against me more.

"Yes, yes," she chanted, urging me on as I withdrew and thrust back in with significant force.

It felt like the whole bed was moving with each thrust, but I only focused on her ass and how it felt beneath my hands as I gripped it. Her legs began to tremble, and I knew I was close to completely losing control. Pulling her body up, I sealed my lips to hers for a searing kiss before letting go so I could slam into her one more time. My hands felt permanently attached to her hips, and I wondered briefly if there would be fingerprints left behind. As much as I didn't like to think of hurting her, the caveman part of me liked that I'd marked her as mine somehow.

Rearing back, I withdrew completely, lining myself up as I thrust in, feeling my balls draw up as I came with a roar. If these rooms weren't sound-proofed, I was confident someone would be breaking in to make sure no one was hurt by how loud my shout was.

Her body trembled beneath me, the aftershocks coursing through her, and I slowly withdrew, falling to the bed with a groan. After a few seconds of panting, I opened my eyes once the blood had returned to my brain. I found Finley with her head tossed back as she rode Cohen, a look of pure ecstasy on her face and one I wanted to be cemented in my brain for all eternity. She looked free, happy, and sexually pleased. Something I hoped to always bring to her life.

Sliding off the bed, I carefully pulled off the condom and walked to the bathroom to dispose of it. Washing my hands, I quickly glanced in the mirror, finding my own eyes not far from Fin's. If I looked even a percentage of what she had, it only reaffirmed that this was the right course for us.

Walking back into the room, I grabbed the discarded shorts and slid them on. Glancing at Milo, I found him captivated by the show as he watched their bodies entwined intensely. I was impressed he didn't pleasure himself. The most he was doing was rubbing his erection outside his shorts, but everything was still on. Maybe he was shy, and I needed to give him some space.

Finley came again a few seconds later, and I walked back into the bathroom, warming the water as I ran a rag under it. When I walked back into the room, she was lying on the bed, a blissed-out expression on her face. Nodding to Cohen as he headed into the bathroom, I gently wiped the washcloth over her, hoping to soothe her. She moaned in relief, and I laid it on her.

Moving to climb off the bed, Fin caught my hand, pulling me back to the mattress. "Thank you, Asa. You're the best."

Grinning, I kissed her and covered her with a blanket before standing and walking out into the kitchen. I didn't know what Milo would do, but it felt like he could use a moment alone with her. Cohen joined me a minute later and worked with me to pick up the trash from lunch. Our space wasn't huge, so keeping it clean felt crucial to not losing our minds all living together.

"You good?" Cohen asked as we sat down on the couch a while later.

"With what occurred in the bedroom or the mission?"

Cohen lifted one corner of his mouth in response. "Both, I guess."

"I'm perfectly okay with the bedroom and feel ready for the mission. Any pointers?"

Cohen seemed to think it over for a few seconds but then shook his head. "Not really. You have good instincts. So follow them."

Nodding, we drifted off into silence as we relaxed. It felt like no time had passed when Milo poked his head out, holding up his phone.

"Thirty-minute warning."

With that, Cohen and I stood, heading to finish getting dressed. It was time to find out if we were Order material or not.

Nine

FINLEY

SITTING in the van running surveillance was boring, especially with Guzman as my companion. My fingers itched to do more, my leg bouncing up and down while I scanned footage. I'd been honest earlier when I said I was okay with staying back; it had made the most sense. But doing it sucked monkey balls.

The need to be the one on the front line coursed through me and I wondered if I had control issues. My brother seemed to think so. He reminded me every time I took over any event, deeming his skills lacking. Okay, maybe he had a point. But it didn't mean I was wrong about his ribbon curls.

Snorting, I focused back on the screen, knowing I needed to be the best lookout for Milo and Asa. Lord knew Guzman wasn't going to do it. He was currently crunching some chips and watching golf on ESPN. I wouldn't let us fail because I was bored… Okay, *jealous*. I didn't like being the lookout. There, I'd said it.

"How's it looking, Oblivion?" Cohen asked, using my code name over the comms, ignoring Guzman. Ryker had developed the app we'd used years ago into a more sophisticated one. With Bluetooth and smartwatches, it was practically seamless now.

"Clear so far. They've moved into position."

"Good, keep me updated." I could hear the apprehension in his voice, and I knew he at least understood how I was feeling. He hated being left behind to watch from the sidelines.

I zoomed in as I watched the three approaching the fire escape. Asa stayed back, manning surveillance from the ground as Milo and Nicole began to climb up. There was an air vent there where they were going to gain access, and shimmy their way down into the bakery. The place had been closed for an hour, and there hadn't been any movement or light since, giving them a fair chance at not running into anyone.

"We've made it to the roof," Nicole said, coming over the comms, slightly out of breath. I switched one of my screens to get a better view, keeping Asa on another. My heart rate started to increase as I watched them, worry for their well-being overcoming me. I couldn't lose them.

Keeping my eyes peeled, I watched as Milo and Nicole opened the vent and put on the rappelling equipment before shimmying down. Their helmets had mini cameras, so I turned them on, finding them as they began to descend into the bakery.

"Holy shit. I didn't think things like this existed," Nicole said, tilting her head down to show us.

Red lasers spread across the room. This bakery had better security than most banks.

"Um, Chaos," I said, switching comms so the team wouldn't hear. "We might have a problem."

I sent him the live feed, his curse letting me know he got it.

"Shit. This wasn't in our surveillance."

"What do we do?" I asked, keeping my gaze focused on Nicole.

"Unless the book is out in the open and one of you is a gymnast, I don't think you're prepared to disable that type of security."

I could hear the disappointment in his voice, and I wondered what it meant for The Order. But I couldn't think that way. This was real; I wouldn't leave my teammates in a bad situation. Switching back to Nicole, I knew what I needed to do.

"Okay, guys, I just need a few minutes to see if I

can disable it. Are you okay with hanging there for a few minutes? Maybe see if you can spot the book?"

"Yeah, sure," Nicole said, and I minimized the camera screen. If Guzman was reliable, I'd have him monitor them, but since he was currently snoring, I didn't feel like putting my faith in him. I'd just have to be quick.

Pulling up the security system website, I cracked my knuckles as I logged in. Cohen had given me one of the most advanced encryption keys earlier, so I was eager to play with it. I just needed to get around the interface and firewall.

Quicker than I thought possible, I made it past the mainframe and began to scroll through the accounts. Earlier, we'd found one, and I disabled it, but this had to be separate since the lasers were still lighting up the room.

Everything had been in a woman's name so far, and I realized that was our mistake. For the legal stuff, it was all in her name. But I bet these lasers weren't on the business plan or budget proposal. No, these were paid with a different account and books, since that was what they protected.

Looking at the file, I found the man's name—Frankie Jacks.

Scrolling through with that name in mind, I smiled when I found what I was looking for a second later. Clicking on his account, I wasn't surprised that his password and two-factor authentication were more complex.

Maximizing the screen, I checked that the others were still okay and clicked on the comms. "I found the system. I just need a minute to deactivate it. You guys, okay?"

A loud rumble started far off, and I cursed, knowing that our time was running out.

"Um, you might want to hurry. I think that's them."

Minimizing the cameras, I focused on the security system, knowing I couldn't be distracted at the moment, or we'd all be toast. My brow began to sweat as I punched in the code to reroute the two-factor so Frankie wouldn't get a notification. Once I had the code to decrypt everything set, I scanned it quickly, afraid I was missing something. The rumble grew louder, and I knew it was now or never.

Striking the key, I watched as the code flew across the screen, praying it would work. When it beeped green, granting me access, I stared at it for a second, convinced I was seeing things.

The rumble reminded me I was out of time, so I quickly clicked the cameras as I shouted into the feed.

"Go, you have maybe sixty seconds before the bikes are on you."

As I said that, I found them touching down into the bakery and running over to the drawer the book was supposed to be placed in. It felt a little too easy that there wasn't a giant safe, but I was guessing Frankie felt secure enough with his lasers to leave it unprotected. It made me wonder if the girlfriend was involved or if she was innocent in all of this. Lasers were easier to hide than a giant safe.

The noise outside grew louder, and I encouraged Nicole and Milo as they began to make their way back up. Quicker than I thought possible, they were up and climbing out of the hole. That was when I realized that Asa had climbed up there with them and had pulled them up quicker. Together, the three placed the vent back and removed their equipment just as the motorcycles made it to the parking lot.

Jolting, I reversed the sequence, setting the lasers and the alarm back on, praying I bought them enough time before the bikers realized we'd been there. Watching the front, I kept my eyes peeled on the three guys as they headed toward the door.

"Once they're in the building, you'll have a short window to get off the roof and book it," I whispered, too worried my voice would carry over their comms.

I watched as they nodded, affirming that they'd

heard me. I glanced back down, glad that the bikers seemed to be here for a regular visit, their chatter and manner relaxed. Once the door was unlocked and they were all through the doors, I shouted the all-clear.

"Now!"

The three of them began to climb over the edge, Asa going first, then Nicole with Milo last. I couldn't help but feel pride that they'd put her in the middle, trying to give her some protection. Though I doubted she needed it with how badass she was, it made me love my guys' thoughtfulness. The door jingled open, and I sucked in a breath.

"Freeze."

Their movement stopped, and I could hear their breathing as they waited. One of the bikers looked to go to his bike, grabbing something out of his saddlebag before returning to the store. Once he was in, I hurried them down the rest of the way. Just as Milo's feet hit the pavement, sounds of disorder erupted from inside as things began to be turned over.

"Go! You don't have long." They quickly took off around the building, and I let out a breath as they ran out of view, finally safe from the men inside. I kept my eyes glued to the bakery, watching the bikers as I waited for my team to reconvene with me. I was parked a couple blocks over, so it would take them a few minutes.

Switching back to Cohen's channel, I was preparing to tell him we were safe when I heard a conversation. I instantly knew I shouldn't listen, but the fact that Ryker and Cohen were talking had me unable to switch off.

"Your team is looking good," Ryker said, and I could almost picture him crossing his arms, his smile smug as he made that statement like he was responsible.

"They are, but it's not because of you," Cohen said, echoing my thoughts.

Ryker sighed, the sound filled with an emotion I couldn't quite place. "If I need to say I'm sorry again, I will Cohen. I was an asshole with no clue how to deal with my own emotions. I panicked and punished you for them. That wasn't fair."

I wished I could see Cohen's face to know what he was feeling right then. The words felt true from Ryker, and I knew it would go a long way toward Cohen forgiving him, but I wasn't sure if it was enough.

"I appreciate that, but it's in the past now. I'd like to move forward in our working relationship and keep it civil."

"Is that all you want?" Ryker asked, his voice

quiet, and I wondered if he was too scared to voice what he really wanted in life.

"Yes," Cohen said, but I didn't quite believe him. The door to the van started to open, jolting me out of my eavesdropping, and I clicked a button, trying to make it sound like I had just come on.

"The team has returned to the van and successfully completed our mission. Headed back to base," I said, keeping it brief since I knew Ryker was there.

Cohen cleared his throat. "Excellent. You've all shown great skills tonight and the ability to adapt to the circumstances. And if I'm not mistaken, you're the first team done. Looks like you four are Order material. See you back at base."

I smiled, not missing how he only said four of us. It felt nice that, for once, our group had been accredited the work we'd done, and the one member hoping to coast on our coattails wouldn't be able to.

I turned around, finding Asa and Milo beaming at me. Jumping up, I wrapped them both in hugs, needing to feel that they were safe more than I was willing to admit. They both briefly kissed me, their hands touching me, and I wondered if they'd been concerned even with me stuck on surveillance.

"That was some fast thinking with the security system. You saved our ass," Milo said, beaming at me.

"Yeah, I thought we were toast," Nicole added, pulling a sweatshirt over her head. The rest of us also changed, making our appearance different in case we'd been picked up on a camera or were pulled over; we wouldn't look the same as whatever description they had. All of my disguises were coming in handy again.

Asa jumped out after he was dressed like a hippie surfer and took the magnet off the side of the van that had advertised tanning oil and put up one for floral arrangements. He got into the driver's side behind the wheel, and I felt my body relax entirely as we made it a few blocks without any trouble.

When he took a turn a little harder than necessary, I tried to contain my laugh when Guzman fell out of his chair and smacked his head. He jerked upright, confused for a second, and then pretended he hadn't been asleep. I didn't want to break it to him that he hadn't passed. I would let Ryker or Cohen be the ones to share that news.

Milo pulled me between his legs onto the floor, and I snuggled back into his arms, liking that he was becoming more comfortable with touching me. I guess seeing me get railed by two of my other boyfriends earlier opened the door more for physical touch. My cheeks heated at the memory, but I couldn't argue I wasn't a fan of how it had turned out.

Laying back against him, I closed my eyes, glad we'd made it through. I wasn't sure which I preferred now since, in the end, being in the van hadn't been as dull as I'd initially imagined. Though, part of me knew I'd always prefer to be on the front line, the need to control the outcome more in my grasp.

Yeah, yeah, I'd admit to being a control freak, and I was learning to be okay with that.

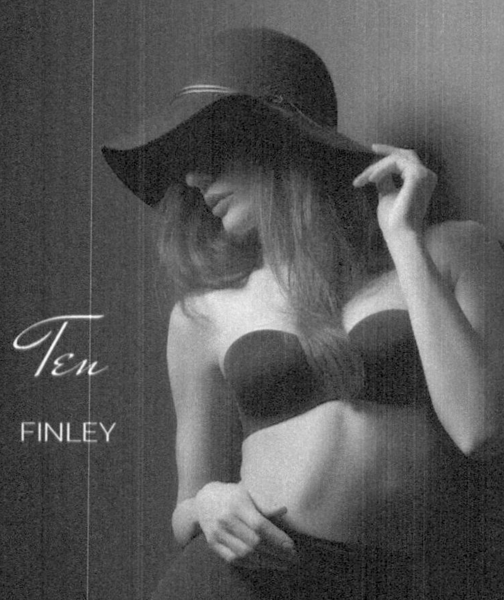

FINLEY

COHEN AND RYKER were waiting for us when we returned. I couldn't make out Ryker's expression, but Cohen had a massive grin on his face, and it was all aimed at me. As soon as I stepped off the elevator, he swooped forward, picking me up into his arms.

"I'm so proud of you," he whispered. "You were amazing and the team leader they needed."

His words fell over me, taking me back. Leader? I hadn't been a leader. I was the non-valuable one on the sidelines.

Cohen watched my face, his eyes narrowing at whatever he saw play across it. "Yes, leader, sweetheart. It takes leadership to know your strengths and how to use them the best instead of just wanting to be the hero. But you were still that in the end with that fast code-breaking. I'm unsure if anyone else could've managed that in the time you did. The motorcyclists were another unforeseen hurdle, but you tackled it together."

He set me down on my feet, looking at the rest of the group. I caught Ryker's eye just before he turned his head, and I wondered if he'd been watching us.

"Great job, Team Campbell. You've all earned a night off from night watch. You can pick which one you'd like. Just let me know so I can alert the others to the schedule." He spun to leave, stopping in his tracks. He gaze flicked to Guzman. "Except you. You're out."

The big brute began to protest, but two guards headed toward him, one a little more aggressive than the other, and I wondered if that was his brother. He didn't look too happy with his younger bro if it was.

We all waited until he was escorted off the grounds and let out a cheer, laughter spilling out as the adrenaline continued to pump through us.

"You guys aren't bad. I'll catch you later," Nicole said, waving as she walked off and joined a group of people playing cards at one of the tables.

As one, we all headed toward our room. I didn't know if they were as eager as I to debrief together or just needed to not feel like we had eyes on us, but I was itching to change clothes and relax. And definitely keep ignoring the thing Cohen said.

Stepping into the suite, I headed for the bedroom, a change of clothes the first thing on my mind. An arm stopped me, and I turned, finding Asa watching me.

"Where are you going, babe?"

"I just want to change clothes. I'll be right out. Promise."

He looked down at his own attire, a grimace forming on his lips. "Yeah, okay, good call."

Laughing, I took his hand, dragging him with me. Pulling out a few things, I quickly realized I needed to do laundry again. I didn't want to admit I might be a bit high maintenance when it came to clothes, but only having about eight outfits was torture.

Asa and I changed and gathered all the dirty clothes scattered around the room from over the week, placing them in the basket. "Why do I feel like this is about to become my life? Always doing laundry?" I joked.

"We could all just walk around naked and eliminate the need for clothes," Cohen offered, stepping into the room as he unbuttoned his shirt. I smirked, licking my lips, liking where this was headed.

"Um, there was a pizza at the door," Milo interrupted, holding the box like he wasn't sure what to make of it.

"Have you never seen a pizza before?" I asked,

wondering just how rich he was. He'd been at the hotel when we ordered one for his graduation, so that couldn't be why he was looking at us strangely.

An uncharacteristic smirk grew on Milo's face, and I stopped, getting hot for a whole new reason. He peered at me from behind his glasses, and I felt like I should be saying, *"Yes, doctor, please check me there."*

"It's the note on top of it that I didn't know how to take, not the pizza itself," he sassed, his eyebrow lifting and making me wonder if he could suddenly read my mind and knew exactly what I'd been thinking.

My face heated, and I walked closer, wishing I had my glasses on so I could mess with them to take his stare off my face. Grabbing the envelope, I slid out the card and read it aloud.

"Thought I'd put the note on the outside this time so you wouldn't accuse me of tampering with it. I remembered how much you liked to eat pizza after a mission. Hope that's still the case. You did well tonight, little hacker. Ryker."

I looked up, taking in the expressions of the others. It seemed like they were waiting for me to respond. Even Cohen had a curious look on his face, and I had to guess the conversation I overheard had helped with the thaw between them.

"He's not wrong, and I'm suddenly starved."

"Ryker had to request that earlier since the kitchen closed two hours ago," Cohen said.

The importance of that statement wasn't lost on me. He knew we'd succeed and had thought ahead to get me a pizza.

Barnacles! He was breaking through my exterior and hitting me right in the mushy heart region.

"Who wants some pizza?" I placed the envelope on the dresser, picked up the laundry basket, and followed Milo. "Um, if you want to change, I'll throw some clothes in the wash."

"Oh, sure."

While I waited for him to return, I grabbed a slice, eating it as I thought. Never before had a piece of pizza felt like it held so much meaning.

"Want some help?" Cohen asked, the basket already in his hands.

"Yeah, that'd be nice." Wiping my hands and face, I walked out of the suite toward the laundry room with him. We were quiet as we made our way. I was lost in my thoughts, trying to put together the puzzle that my dating life was suddenly.

Separating colors and delicates, I went through the motions as I added the laundry detergent and softener. It wasn't until I hit the start button that Cohen even tried to talk.

"How are you feeling? You seem deep in your head."

When faced with a question you weren't prepared to answer, the best course of action was a deflection.

"I overheard your conversation with Ryker," I blurted instead.

Cohen smiled, moving forward to block and back me up against the washer. He braced his hands on the top, leaning over me as he stared down at me with his intense eyes.

"I know. I wanted you to hear. The comms beep when a new party enters the channel."

"Oh." I swallowed, licking my lips, trying to think of what to say. "I'm still sorry I didn't say anything."

"What did you think of what he had to say?"

"He sounded remorseful. I actually wanted to talk to you about that, but you're making it hard to think with you standing over me like this," I gasped, my eyes shuttering as his lips grazed my cheek.

"Is that so? I kind of like having you at my mercy." He moved back, placing his hands on my hips, and lifted me up to sit on the washer. "But this is important, and I think we need to have this conversation."

He stepped back, leaning against the other side, and I instantly missed him. So much so that a little whine left me, causing him to grin. Cohen stepped forward, and I wrapped my legs around his waist, liking the physical contact with him. My hands began to run through his hair and his eyes closed as he leaned against my arm.

"At first, seeing and learning who he was in my life was shocking. But after I had time to think about it, I realized that he hadn't been as awful as I made him out to be. Ryker hadn't promised me anything, but my young heart was in love, so it felt like a tragic betrayal. Knowing he's been watching over me shifts that a little. I wasn't always open with you about my feelings, so I can understand his actions a little more. I don't know if I want to be in a relationship with him anymore, but I think I can forgive him and find a way to be friends and colleagues where I don't want to punch him every five seconds."

Chuckling, I kept playing with his hair and massaging his scalp. It seemed to be the perfect balance of us being vulnerable without it being too scary.

"I know what you mean. I can recognize the fact that he wasn't the one to set me up now, and those feelings I had for him never really went away, but it's hard to trust when I've been jilted. When I was not so secretly listening, I had an epiphany that no matter what happens with Ryker, I think it's a decision we must make together. Because I don't want to lose you. You're my heart, Co-bear."

"Finley Amelia Reyes, don't you know how much I love you? A stupid amount." He grinned, his eyes so full of love that I practically melted.

"Stupid amount, huh? I could almost take that as an insult."

"I told you I love you for the second time, and you're worried about the fact I said stupid?" His brow creased as he tried to work it out.

"I love you a stupid amount, too," I said, my cheeks heating. Cohen stopped, the biggest smile ever crossing his face.

"Say it again, sweetheart. I wasn't prepared."

Swallowing, I braced my hands on his face, and he closed his eyes for half a second as my thumbs smoothed over his cheeks. "I love you, Cohen Campbell. A stupid amount."

"It's Michael. My middle name is Michael."

Smiling, I leaned forward, kissing him. My legs tightened around his waist, and I pulled him closer. His arousal met my core as our kiss became frenzied. We made out like teenagers and it was only the buzzer going off twenty minutes later reminding us that the clothes were done that stopped us from going further.

Laughing, I pulled back, leaving his hair a mess

from my fingers. My face tingled from his stubble, and my panties felt damp, but I didn't care in the slightest. I felt full and happy, the feeling I'd been pretending to be for so long.

Jumping down, we both switched our loads into the dryer and then walked back to the room, hand in hand. The machines were connected to an app that would notify us when they were finished. Asa and Milo were spread out on the couches when we walked back into the suite, watching a movie. They smiled at me when we entered, and Asa stood to warm up some pizza.

In our conversation, I'd forgotten all about food. I guess there were some things more important than pizza, after all. Huh.

Sitting on the couch, I relaxed between Asa and Milo with a piece of pizza on my lap. "What are you watching?" I asked, lifting it up to my lips. Cohen chose to sit in front of the couch, pulling my legs over his shoulders so he could keep touching me.

"Just some movie on TV. Do you want to watch something different? We were too tired to choose."

I realized it was *Sweet Home Alabama*, so I shook my head, liking this one. The guys fell into a comfortable silence as we all relaxed, giving way to decompressing from the night. When the app buzzed a while later, Milo and Asa were both passed out on the couch.

"Looks like it's bedtime. I'll grab the clothes if you get them to move to the bed?" Cohen suggested. Sighing, I laughed, knowing it would be easier to get the laundry but letting Cohen have this one.

Gently, I woke both of them up, and surprisingly they got up without any issue, heading to the bedroom. I waited until Cohen returned and helped him fold the clothes and hang the ones that needed to be. As we finished, I smiled at the domesticated bliss we'd seemed to have found amongst ourselves, and I realized just how much I liked it. A girl could get used to this.

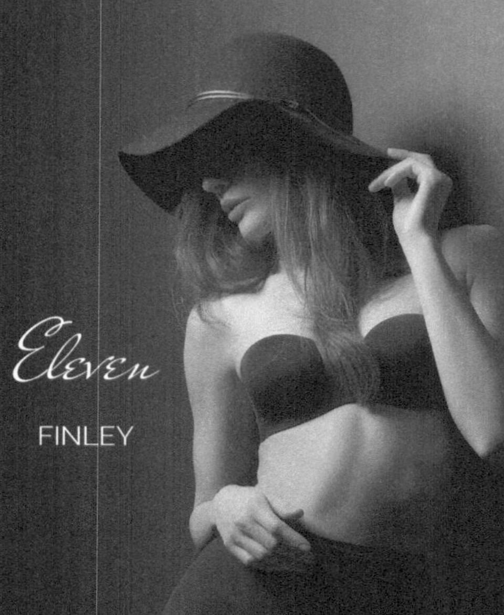

Eleven

FINLEY

THE NEXT WEEK consisted of training sessions ranging from physical workouts or combat in the morning to learning a skill in the afternoon to evening. I'd perfected my lock-picking ability, worked on some new code, and gained muscle I never thought I'd have. I still hated running, but at least now I wasn't dying after a mile. In fact, I'd completed five miles today. It felt nice to achieve something, and like maybe I could defend myself at the end of this.

Ryker had been there through it all like an over-protective guardian. He was always watching, but out of reach. I didn't know if he was purposefully holding himself back or not wanting to cross lines while we were in training. The rest of us were growing closer in the meantime.

Nicole had been paired up with us on other missions, and thankfully none of them had been as stressful or down to the wire as the first one. I'd heard some rumblings that the only reason we were doing well was because of my relationship with Cohen. Still, I ignored them, knowing that, if anything, we were being held to a higher standard because of our relationship. Not the other way around. People would talk no matter what, especially whenever you did something well.

That was the thing I was learning about jealousy. Everybody was jealous over something, and some people would do whatever they could to take what you had. I'd worked hard to get to this point, fighting my demons and earning my retribution. There was only one obstacle left in my way of having the future I wanted. People who didn't even know me or my journey wouldn't be able to take that from me. Not now.

"Guess what?" Cohen asked, walking into the suite.

"What?" I looked up from my phone, finding him smiling at me. I'd been scrolling through photos of my brother and Sawyer's latest costumes, and I hated them. Unfortunately, there wasn't much I could do being this far away, so I was trying to think of a nice way to send my recommendations to the designer.

"Everything okay?" he asked, stopping what he'd been about to tell me. I guess I hadn't masked my frustration as well as I thought.

"It's nothing. What were you going to tell me?" I placed my phone down and looked at him with my big doe eyes. Cohen sat on the couch, taking my hand. He smiled at me, and I melted. Gah, he was too cute.

"I just secured you and one person a pass off the base."

I sat up straighter, intrigued by what this could mean. "Oh, and what would I get to do with this pass off the base?" I asked as excitement filled my voice. It wasn't that I didn't like it here. The Order had everything possible that you could want, from food to entertainment, exercise, and even a bar. But the one thing they didn't have was a clothing store. I was this close to making my childhood dream come true and finding some random fabric that wasn't being used, to make clothes. I felt that desperate.

Cohen lifted his eyebrows, giving me a look. "A trip to the mall, if one wanted," he said nonchalantly like it wasn't the best news ever.

Shrieking, I jumped up, waving my hands as I ran around the couch. "Please tell me you're serious. This is not something to joke about, Co-bear."

Smirking, he stood and stopped my waving

hands by placing his on my hips. He leaned forward and gave me a gentle kiss on the forehead.

"Oh, believe me, sweetheart. This is not something I would joke about when it comes to you. And as much as I would like to be the one to earn this. I think you should take Milo."

"Really?" I asked, surprised he would offer this chance to get off the base to someone else.

"Yeah, I'm learning that being in this relationship means that sometimes there are sacrifices, and I can admit that Asa and I have had more opportunities and time with you. And if Milo is going to feel more part of the bro club, then he needs alone time with you. And that's really hard to do while we're shoved underground at this base. So, use your pass wisely. Besides, I think he would probably enjoy shopping the most anyway. The guy seems like the type to enjoy that stuff." He shrugged like it wasn't a big deal, but I heard it for what it was.

"You just don't want to carry all my bags.," I teased, appreciating the sentiment of what he was giving up.

He snorted but pulled me a little closer, leaning down to whisper, "I'd carry all your bags at the snap of your little finger, but I know Milo needs time with you. Don't ever doubt I wouldn't spend every waking second with you, sweetheart."

He kissed my cheek, stepping back, leaving me all hot and bothered to go and tell Milo. Fanning myself, I squeezed his butt cheek as I skipped off to the other bedroom.

Milo was lying on the bed, flipping through a book. He looked up when I entered, and I smiled as I leaned against the frame, checking him out. Now that I could, I wanted to do it all the time. He watched me, a curious look on his face. He'd grown more comfortable with us over the week and a half here, and I loved that he was part of this.

"Hey, cutie," I said, smiling widely. "Would you like to go on a date with me?"

He pushed up his glasses as he sat up. "A date?" he asked. I couldn't tell from the distance, but it looked like his cheeks were reddening.

"Yep. Can you be ready in 10 minutes?"

"Yeah, sure. Where are we going?"

"Just to the mall. Cohen was able to get me a pass knowing how much I was dying without more clothes. And now that I don't have to hide from everybody, I can pay you back."

"You don't have to do that, Fin. I did it because I wanted to help you."

"I know. It's just—"

He cut me off, standing. "No, I have more money than I need. The fact I got to help a friend meant something to me. So please, it will hurt my heart if you were to deny me that gift by paying me back." He placed his hands in a begging motion, and I realized this was more than about money. "I understand you're not like other girls and just expect it of me. I know that. That's not what I think about you at all. This was more about me needing to feel like I was doing something different from my family and that I was making a difference. So please," he begged some more. Milo had walked closer with his speech, imploring me with his eyes.

I swallowed, gulping down the words I'd been about to say. "Okay," I agreed, realizing how much he needed this. I wasn't going to be a brat about it. "Thank you." I leaned up and kissed his lips.

"Now. Date time." I smiled widely, and his shoulders dropped when I didn't argue. "I'll see you in a few."

I walked into the other room to grab some clothes. While we all tended to sleep in here together, every now and then, one of the guys would go and sleep in the other bed. I understood it. It was a bit cramped and uncomfortable with four people in the bed. So, they'd rotate out every few days. They'd also moved all of their clothing to that room when they realized how stressed out it made me. I quickly dressed in some skinny jeans, a flowy top, a jean jacket, and my

Chucks, since we'd be walking a lot. I instantly felt chipper getting out of my everyday yoga pants I'd been wearing for training with the knowledge of where we were headed at the forefront of my mind.

I wouldn't deny I was a girl who enjoyed shopping. I loved finding hidden gems along with the allure of getting something new. It instantly made me happier. The bonus was getting to spend alone time with Milo. I knew how precious time was here.

I walked out into the main area, finding Asa and Cohen standing together at the sink. Asa spotted me first and grabbed my hands as he checked me out from head to toe. He made a wolf whistle, causing my cheeks to heat.

"Fin, you look amazing. I'm kind of jealous now that I'm not going."

"What are you and Cohen going to do?" I asked.

"I think we're going to head down and play some pool. I'm going to see if Ryker is available, too. I think they could use some time to just hang out where they aren't working and maybe... without you as a distraction. "

I chuckled, but he wasn't wrong. He gave me a kiss, making my toes curl in my shoes. I reluctantly pulled away before things became too hot, and I didn't make it out of here. There were only a few things that would tempt me away from one of my lovers. And shopping was one of them. Chuckling, Asa smacked my butt and pushed me over to Cohen to say goodbye. It amazed me how comfortable we'd all grown with touching and kissing in front of each other.

Cohen gave me one of his saucy looks, quickly kissing me and telling me to be safe. When I finished my goodbyes, I found Milo standing, waiting for me. He wore a soft smile, making my heart race.

"You ready?" he asked.

I nodded, walking to take his hand. We headed out to the elevator, meeting our escort—a guard. While we were getting let off the base, we wouldn't be completely alone. It helped since I didn't know this area, and having to think about driving down that mountain again made me squeamish. Equally making me glad we had someone doing it for us.

When he drove underground a few minutes later instead of leaving the garage, I looked at Milo, confused. The guard driving chuckled, watching us in the mirror.

"Yeah, they make everybody who arrives the first time come up the mountain, but they built a tunnel underneath that will take you directly down it. You have to have special access to get to it. And until you're in The Order, you're not allowed to know it exists."

The thought of being in a car underground made me feel a little weird but as brilliant as these people were, along with their technology, I had to assume it was safe. Besides, wasn't there a really long tunnel under an ocean overseas? Surely then, a mountain was safer than being underwater. Being underground took us half the time to get down the mountain. Before I knew it, we were pulling out of the tunnel.

I blinked at the daylight, warming my face in the sun. I hadn't seen the actual sun in a week and a half. The Order did such a great job with the digital screens that I almost forgot that it was fake sometimes, but nothing could make you feel like the real sun. That wasn't something you could manufacture.

When we pulled up to the mall a little while later, I was practically bouncing in my seat. Milo laughed at me, but I didn't care. This was truly one of my happy places. The guard said he would follow but keep at a distance, making me like him even more. He'd told us his name was Leo, and he'd been with The Order for thirty years and only worked part-time. It was nice to see people respecting their organization enough to dedicate their lives to it.

Milo and I soon forgot about his presence as we began walking through the mall, and I pointed at everything. When I headed into a store, I became dizzy with all the new things and colors. I felt a little like Pretty Woman as I started trying on outfits, and Milo waited outside the fitting room for me. He would clap and give me a compliment for each outfit.

"Get them all," he said at one point, but I shook my head. It was fun to imagine them all, but I didn't need this many clothes. I might be a fashionista, but I was also practical.

I ended up getting quite a few, and it made him happy to give them to me. In turn, it made me doubly happy.

Oh wow, I was beginning to sound like such a sap.

I convinced him to buy some clothes for himself, and we picked a few things for Cohen and Asa. They didn't need too many things since most of our time was spent in loose-fitting athletic wear, but it never hurt to be prepared. Plus, I liked knowing that we had a choice. It didn't feel quite as prison-esque that way. For some reason, that was my unit of measure. Nobody could be fashionable in prison.

So, if we could wear different things, then it couldn't be all that bad. Loose association, but I never claimed to make sense.

"I'm starved. Want to grab something to eat?" I asked Milo, who was laden down with bags. He nodded his head in the affirmative, and I glanced over at the guard, who was also carrying bags. He shrugged. I guess I'd stolen their voices with all of my purchases.

"We still have a little bit of time left." My stomach grumbled, and I realized how hungry I was, so we headed to the Food Court as a group. They let me go first and then took turns grabbing food, so someone was always at the table with all of our stuff. I realized I might've gone a little overboard when it was all stacked together.

When we all had our food, we dug in, the already limited conversation going away. Maybe that was why we didn't notice what was happening at first, too consumed by our food and hunger.

When the first scream sounded, I thought it was people excited. But as chairs and tables began to be pushed aside, falling to the ground, I realized something more sinister was at play. The screams grew louder, and I could hear the fear as people ran in every direction. Leo jumped into action, turning and looking for the cause. I had a feeling he wouldn't find a person.

If this was MKG and Dex, then they would be smarter than being out in the open.

Just as I thought that a bullet whizzed past our table, hitting one of the bags. Shrieking, I dove for the floor, pulling Milo with me. My body trembled as I searched for my phone, wanting to call somebody. I hit the first name that I saw, praying the phone would ring. As it became quieter around me, I grew even more scared of what that meant. When the call dropped a moment later, I knew his next round of attack had been implemented.

He was taking out the cell phones, so no one could call for help, making us stuck.

I turned to Milo, my eyes wide with fear. He looked as lost and scared as me, as we gripped one another.

"What do we do now?" I asked just as a loud bang erupted close by. Milo froze as well, his answer dying on his lips.

Everything in our training fled me, and I squeezed my eyes shut as my heart began to race, my breathing becoming shallow. I didn't want to pass out, but my brain was overloaded, and I couldn't think. I didn't want to die. I was stupid to bring the guys into this. I should've just left it alone and lived out my life. I could've kept pretending.

But as my panic swirled, I knew that wasn't fair. This could've happened regardless, and I wouldn't want to give up the time I had with these guys for a chance I might avoid this. No. I needed to calm down and focus.

I'd been trained, so I just needed to use it.

Milo squeezed my fingers, reassuring me, and I

looked up, nodding that we'd get through this together. I wasn't alone, and Milo was great at rescuing me. So, maybe it was time we helped these innocent people.

I took a deep breath when he placed a gun in my hand. Holding his eyes, so many emotions passed through them, and I shook my head, not wanting a goodbye.

I kissed him, not letting him say anything, just as a voice came out over the speaker system.

"Come out, come out, Oblivion. No one else has to get hurt."

Twelve

MILO

A SHRILL RINGING SOUNDED in my ears, and I blinked, trying to understand what was happening. Fin trembled next to me, the gun shaking in her hand. I needed to focus. The guys had trusted me to keep her safe, and I'd do that at whatever cost.

The PA system came on again, sending a shiver down my spine. "Now, now, Oblivion. It doesn't have to be this difficult. Maybe I should up the stakes?"

A gunshot sounded out, followed by a scream. I tensed, expecting it to hit us next. Sobbing was the only sound I could hear; everything else in the once loud mall was quiet. Too quiet.

I looked around for Leo, spotting his leg a few tables over. Things we'd purchased were scattered around the floor between us.

"Leo?" I whispered.

When he didn't move, I feared the worst. Swallowing, I nodded to Fin that I would check him out. I peered over the table, not seeing anyone standing. Staying crouched, I moved over to him, slumping down behind the table. I could see Finley from the angle as she bit her lip, watching me.

Taking a breath, I prepared myself to look at Leo. He was sprawled out, blood seeping from a wound on his shoulder. My medical instincts kicked in, and I placed the gun down as I immediately began to address his injury. I found an exit wound, making it easier to manage. Ripping off part of his shirt, I applied pressure as I searched for something to use.

Grabbing one of the new tops Fin had just bought, I pressed it onto the spot and grabbed a thong that had fallen out; using the elastic, I tied it around the shirt, holding it in place. Taking Leo's pulse, I found it beating, if not a little slow. Slapping his face, I tried to stir him. I needed to know what the protocol in this type of situation was.

"Leo," I hissed, slapping him again. It seemed to work, and he opened his eyes, looking at me. "Is there an emergency protocol? Cell phones are down."

He blinked, coming to. "Wa-tch."

Understanding, I placed his gun in his hand and peeked over the table, still not spotting anyone.

Moving back over, I slumped against the back of the table as I caught my breath. Fin squeezed my arm, her eyes boring into mine.

"He said there's something on the watch that should alert the others," I whispered. Or at least I hoped that was what he meant, and it wasn't an instant kill switch. Fin nodded, looking down at hers as she typed into it.

"Time's up, Oblivion. Another one bites the dust. I'll keep killing people until you show yourself."

The gunshot was closer this time, as was the scream. Fin tensed, her hands trembling as she began to shake her head. I knew what she was thinking, but there was no way I'd let her sacrifice herself.

"No. You can't give yourself up, Fin. It won't solve anything."

Her lip trembled as she stared at me, and I swiped away a tear, leaving a trail of blood behind. "What do you need?" I asked, deciding the best course was to focus on what we could do.

"If I had access to a computer, I could tap into the cameras and find him. But unless it's wired into the system, I doubt I'll have any luck since he's blocking the signal."

"Okay, so that makes it difficult, but not impossi- ble," I said, thinking through possibilities.

"The security booth would have surveillance!"

she said, some life coming back to her. "First, I need to tap into the code on these watches to send an alert." She fiddled with her watch as I looked around, spotting a few more people who seemed to be in need. Looking around at all the food places, I spotted a first aid kit on a shelf.

"I'll be right back," I whispered, crawling away before she could stop me. I stopped every few feet to hide and reached the last table before I'd be out in the open. Looking back, I peered around again, not spotting anyone. I wasn't sure where he was shooting from, but it didn't seem like he was close.

Taking a deep breath, I prayed I'd live long enough to see Finley naked again. It seemed dumb, but it was the one thing I thought about as I took off at a run, jumping over the counter as I rolled to the floor. I smiled, shocked that it had worked. A few workers were huddled together, looking at me in fear, and I couldn't understand why.

When I lifted my hand, I realized it was because of the gun. Placing it back into a holster, I raised my empty hands. "I'm not the bad guy. I'm a doctor. Is anyone hurt?"

They regarded me for a while before one of them nodded, moving to show me a man on the floor they'd been shielding. Reaching up for the first aid kit, I opened it and began to look through it.

"Shit, I'm going to need more. Can one of you go to the other food places and grab theirs?"

A young boy nodded as his mom began to cry, but she didn't stop him as he hurried off. I felt like an ass, but we'd need the supplies, and he might be the best option to get them. He was small and quick. I got to work, helping the man on the floor who looked to have hit his head.

"I think he has a concussion but should be okay for now." I cleaned his wound and sealed it for the moment. The woman patted my hand, thanking me.

Moving to the side, I was about to make a break for it when the boy returned, three more kits in his arms. Smiling, I took them from him. Taking a chance, I shoved them across the floor, not wanting to hinder my escape with them in my hands.

Once they were all against the table, I took a deep breath and ran for it. A shot rang out, and I cursed, feeling it graze me as I ducked down behind the table. Checking it over, I sighed with relief when I saw it was only a tiny cut. Taking more time than I had, I ducked and weaved my way from person to person, checking them over for injuries. Most of the crowd seemed to be okay, making me relieved that there weren't many dying people without medical attention here.

When I got to another section, I realized that

wasn't the case here. Blood covered the floor, and I slid through it as I moved toward the woman holding a man. I knew before I got there that it wasn't good. There were bullet wounds in his chest and leg, both bleeding profusely. His eyes were closed, and when I checked his pulse, there wasn't one.

"I'm sorry," I said, tears brimming my eyes.

The woman sniffed, nodding. "He saved me. I don't even know his name, but I didn't want him to be alone." I squeezed her hand, feeling like she needed some comfort.

"Psst," a voice said behind me, and I turned to find Fin crouching. She swallowed when she saw the woman and man, her face dropping slightly. She nodded, and I looked back to the woman, but she had her eyes closed as she rocked the man back and forth, her lips moving over a silent prayer.

"I managed to send a message and found the security booth. But…" she trailed off, biting her lip again.

"What?" I asked, already knowing the answer.

"It's all the way over there," she nodded in a direction that was all open space. As I opened my mouth to tell her no, the PA system crackled on again.

"Times up, Oblivion. Another victim to add to your tally. It's beginning to get steep."

Fin squeezed her eyes, her body shaking as a gunshot rang out further away this time. "I have to go. I can't let him keep killing people."

Thoughts of what the others would say raced through my head. Everything in me wanted to protect her, to keep her from this, and I knew they'd want the same. But I couldn't cage, Finley. She was as strong and capable as I was of doing this. Maybe more so. Taking a long, stuttering breath, I opened my eyes and pulled her close to me, kissing her deeply.

"Be safe, Fin." I bit back everything else I wanted to say, hoping by not doing it, I'd have another chance, that the universe might owe me for once, for all the bad shit in my life before her.

"You too," she said, squeezing my hand as she took her own breath before she darted out, heading for the closest cover. A bullet whizzed past her, but she was able to dodge it. I looked in the direction it had come from, but nothing was making sense. Each shot came from a different angle. He either had multiple hidden shooters, or he could move and shoot from various locations without being seen. Neither seemed possible, but my eyes couldn't find a person to make sense of it.

When Fin took off for another section, I held my breath as she made it. She had only one more area before the security office, and then she'd have to open the door. I couldn't stop the shooter, but maybe I could draw their focus away. As she steeled herself for the last leg of her journey, I stood up, taking in the area. I wanted to paint a target on myself and get a lay of the food court, so I knew where to go.

A loud pop sounded next to me, and I ducked back down, yelling as the thing I'd been hiding in front of was filled with bullets. Quickly, I moved over to a new section just as Fin made it into the office. Blood trailed on the ground, and I hoped it wasn't crucial. I couldn't let myself focus on it right now. She had her job to do, and I had mine. I'd seen three more people that needed medical attention when I stood, and I was all they had.

Crawling over, I made it to the first victim and began to clean and dress their wounds. I was down to two first aid kits, making it even more vital that help arrived soon. Over the next few minutes, I zeroed in on what I needed to do and tried to let everything else fade away. Fin would figure this out. I had faith in her.

The second person I came upon looked at me, shaking their head as they pointed to a small child.

"Help… her." I looked over and saw she had been

shot, and I wondered if this person had tried to cover her with their body. MKG might've thought people would turn over Fin to save themselves, but if anything, I saw countless acts of heroism as mere strangers sacrificed themselves for others.

My hands started to shake, and I squeezed my eyes shut as I breathed. Taking out some tweezers, I motioned for the woman to hold the little girl down while I searched for the bullet fragments. The man who'd saved her closed his eyes, happy that she was safe, and I shed a tear for him. Focusing on the little girl, I concentrated, wanting to make his sacrifice worth it.

Finding a few shards, I pulled them out and then used the sewing kit to stitch her up for now. It wasn't ideal, but it would work for the time being. The woman thanked me, tears streaming down her face. Nodding, I wiped my bloodied hands on my jeans, trying to clean them as much as possible as I peeked around for the last person I'd seen.

When I got there, I didn't know where to start. This had to be one of the first victims, as multiple wounds were bleeding. None seemed fatal, but it wouldn't matter if she bled out. Focusing on the worst of the bunch, I cleaned and applied pressure, working through them as I used stitches and pads to hold off the worst of it.

"Thank you," the teenager said, and I prayed that help would be here soon. I didn't know how long these people had if it wasn't.

Slowly, I turned, looking at the door Fin had gone in. It was still closed, with no movement, and I had to believe that meant she was still safe. I debated where to go when the PA system came on again, this time, his voice a little frantic.

"Very well, Oblivion. We'll have to continue our *game* at a later date. I see you've gained some new skills. I'll keep that in mind. Enjoy this parting gift."

Just as he finished, I could make out sirens in the background, my body relaxing, knowing that help was coming. Fin opened the door, a smile on her face, peeking out and looking for danger. I smiled at her, so proud of her for managing to do it.

"You did—"

A loud explosion sounded behind me, throwing me forward, and everything went black.

Thirteen

FINLEY

THE THRILL of cracking Obsidian's position raced through me as I hit some keys. The tricky asshole wasn't even here, but he'd managed to place drones in various places and he was shooting remotely. The jerkwad was still hiding behind his computer somewhere. Tapping into the remote frequency, I used one of the new apps from The Order on my watch and located their positions. Shutting them down, I pumped my arms into the air in victory.

Exhilaration surged through me at having solved this and hopefully saved some more lives. I didn't want to think about the guilt I was sure to feel later.

Cohen: Sweetheart, you okay?
ME: I shut down the drones. We should be clear of danger now. ETA?

Cohen: Soon. Good job, sweetheart.

"Very well, Oblivion. We'll have to continue our game at a later date. I see you've gained some new skills. I'll keep that in mind. Enjoy this parting gift."

With Dex's retreat, I stepped out of the booth, the sound of sirens making my heart slow. We'd made it. We were safe.

Instantly, I spotted Milo, a massive smile on his face. He was covered in blood, and I hoped it wasn't his.

"You did—"

His words were cut off as a massive explosion rocked the space behind him. His body flew forward, and I stumbled from the aftershocks. My heart thumped in my ears as I ran ahead, slipping every few feet on debris and falling rumble. I focused on him, needing to get to Milo.

When I reached his body, I grabbed his wrist, remembering some of the first aid training we'd received. My eyes scanned him, looking for any signs of injury. He had a cut on his head, my free hand shook over it as I debated what to do.

Sound around me ceased to exist. I couldn't hear anything outside of my own heart. Looking up, I saw what I assumed were people moving, but they were blobs, indistinct in color and shape. My mind raced with what steps to take, but I couldn't grab any of it. All it seemed to focus on was that I was going to lose someone. That I was responsible.

Tears fell down my cheeks as I rocked back and forth. I smoothed the hair away from Milo's forehead, praying to whoever would listen to let him live.

"Darling?" a voice croaked, reaching my ears. A hand squeezed mine, and I realized it was Milo's who I was holding.

"Milo?" I asked.

"What… happened?" he whispered, trying to open his eyes.

"Ssh, don't. I'll get you help." I began to look around, my gaze landing on a familiar dark head of hair and dark eyes as they charged toward me. My body sagged in relief as I realized that help had arrived.

"It will be okay, now," I said to Milo to reassure myself as tears fell down my cheeks harder.

"Over here," Ryker shouted, directing an EMT to us. My body shook, and I struggled to let go of Milo. It was only through Ryker's coaxing that they'd be able to give him medical attention, that I could release him.

As soon as he was on the stretcher, Ryker scooped me up and stormed out of the mall with me in his arms. I didn't fight him, not caring about our history any longer. It all seemed so trivial when people's lives were at stake. I buried my head in his arms, no longer feeling the high of defeating Dex at his own game. He might be a coward, but he covered his bases, and I hadn't anticipated that. Ryker carried me outside, and I clung to him, needing to feel safe.

"Ssh, little hacker. You did well. I'll take care of this. I promise. Dex will be held responsible."

I peered up into his eyes, finding them trained on me. They held the promise he spoke of and so much more. Ryker showed me at that moment I could trust him, that I wasn't foolish for doing it. Something in me shifted, and I nodded, my heart slowing as I accepted this.

I wasn't a scared little girl anymore. I'd become strong and wouldn't stop until he was brought to justice. Ryker was telling me I didn't have to do it alone, which felt like the greatest gift.

"Okay," I said. My heart began to settle, my nerves no longer trembling. I wouldn't give in to the fear. He might be a psychotic genius, but he was still a man, which meant he could be defeated.

"I need to go and check over some things. I will leave you with Cohen and meet you at the base. Milo will be taken there and given the best treatment."

Nodding, I watched as he hesitated before lightly pressing a kiss to my forehead, holding me to his chest. "I thought I'd lost you," he whispered so quietly that I almost wondered if I imagined it. Before responding, he set me on my feet, nodding to someone behind me.

"Fin?" Cohen asked, taking my hand. "Let's get you checked out, sweetheart."

I turned to him, my body exhaling at his nearness. Nodding, I wrapped my arms around him, needing to feel his comfort. "Asa?" I asked.

"Right here, babe."

I lifted my head, finding him near, and raised my hand to draw him closer. He came willingly, and the three of us stood in the parking lot in a three-person hug. They both petted my hair, reassuring themselves I was okay.

"Come on, we can get back to the base and check on Milo once you're clear."

They directed me to a paramedic who quickly cleaned and bandaged my cuts, stating I'd need to watch for a concussion, but otherwise, I was injury free. I had a slight sprain to my wrist, but it should heal in a few days. Considering the circumstances, I was lucky.

Asa and Cohen both seemed to exhale in relief at the news. As they began to lead me toward a car, I spotted a familiar face. I turned toward them despite my boyfriend's grumblings.

"Leo?"

He looked up, a faint smile on his face. "Hey, Fin. You okay?" he asked, assessing my injuries.

"Yeah, just a sprain and some minor cuts. How are you?" I nodded to the spot on his arm.

"Alive, thanks to Milo. I was shot, and he saved me. Where is he?" he asked, looking behind me. Tears welled in my eyes, and he caught them, his face falling.

"He was caught in the explosion. I'm not sure how he is. We're headed back now." My lip began to tremble, tears threatening to fall again, but I held them back. I couldn't fall apart here, or I'd never recover.

"He's strong. He'll pull through."

I nodded, hoping Leo was right. Patting his arm, I turned back to Asa and Cohen, taking their hands as they led me to the car. Once inside the vehicle, Asa pulled me into his arms, and I shut my eyes, hoping that things would be different when I woke.

THE MACHINE BEEPED NEXT to me, the sound a steady rhythm to the background noise. It was quiet in the medical wing, only Milo requiring a room. Leo had been brought back here but was gone now. He'd needed stitches but hadn't required surgery for his bullet wound. The doctor credited Milo with saving him.

While we waited for Milo to return from surgery, Ryker called to tell us that all in all, Milo had saved ten people. The death toll was at four, with multiple injured. Two deaths were from the drones, and two from the bomb that had been set off in the shoe store on the corner of the food court. The Order had taken over the investigation, acting as FBI and Homeland security. There wasn't any information released yet to the press, but it was only a matter of time, and I was curious how they would spin it. It made me wonder how many things had been spun my whole life, like Mongoose's murder.

Now, I sat alone next to Milo's bed. He'd been back from surgery for a couple of hours. He'd woken once, but it had been brief. I debated if I should tell someone, but I didn't think outside of us that Milo had any family. None that he talked to anyway.

So, I sat in the quiet room, the heart rate machine my measure of how he was doing. Asa and Cohen had kept me company for a while, but I'd sent them to the room to sleep. Milo was in a stable condition, so there wasn't any need for them to stay here. I just didn't want him to wake up and be alone. My eyes scanned over his frame, taking in each new cut and mark.

He'd been grazed by a few bullets in multiple areas, but it was the burns and slight swelling on the brain they were most concerned with. Milo had come out of surgery well, and the doctor had high hopes for his recovery. Apparently, they had some advanced technology that cut rehab time in half. It was nice to know it wouldn't ruin his plans to start at Lux in the fall if he was able to recover from this. It would be one less thing for me to feel guilty over.

"Stop," a voice said, drawing my eyes to his. His glasses had been knocked off in the explosion, so I wondered how well he could see now without them. His eyes were clear, though, and I could see them without any intrusion.

"Hey," I said, moving closer to peer at him. "How are you doing?"

"Like I've had a whole building fall onto me. Oh, wait." He smiled, the motion looking more like a grimace. Laughing, I wiped a tear, unable to stop them.

"None of that, darling. I'm fine."

"No, you're not." I shook my head, my lip wobbling as I tried to find the words.

Milo lifted his hand, taking mine. With his other, he hit the button to lift the head of his bed up, allowing him to sit up.

"Bring me the chart, will you, darling?"

Sucking in a breath, I dropped his hand, padded over to the wall, and grabbed it. I waved at the nurse outside, and she smiled, returning to her computer. Carrying the folder to Milo, I tried to show a brave face. In reality, all I really wanted to do was curl up in his arms and sleep for a few days. I handed it to him, and he pulled the tray across the bed, surprising me with how well he knew how to operate a medical room.

"I just graduated, Fin. I've been doing clinical rounds for years in med school." He peered at me with a soft smile, easing my guilt.

"Right, doctor." I nodded as he winked. He flipped through it, taking in everything that looked like a foreign language to me.

"Okay, so it's not as bad as you're making it out to be. The way you're going on, I thought I was dying."

"Milo!" I gasped, shocked he'd be so carefree with his words.

"Yes, darling?" His eyes twinkled, and I couldn't reconcile them with him in the hospital bed.

"You could've died!"

"But I didn't. So, who do I need to see to get out of here? I'd prefer to sleep in a bed with you than this."

"But… your injuries! You just had surgery."

"Yes, it was minor, and I've been in recovery for hours. All of my wounds are superficial and have been bandaged. My burns are covered, and I'll need to have them checked out over the next few days, but nothing that requires me to be here. There will be tests to come, I know this, but again, there's nothing that requires me to be in a hospital bed right now."

"He's right," a voice said from the door. I turned to find Ryker standing there. He looked exhausted.

"You okay?" I asked. "Did you find anything?"

"It's been a long day. Can we debrief in the morning? I just came down to see how Milo was doing. The doctor on duty gave me a rundown, saying he'd be free to go once he woke up. He's awake and seems clear-headed to me."

His eyes held mine, emotion swirling in them, and I realized I had to trust them. I didn't know why I was so focused on Milo needing to stay anyway. It was better if he wasn't here. Dropping my shoulders, I walked over to the bag I'd put together and placed it on the bed.

"I brought you some clothes." I kissed his cheek,

walking out of the room to give him some privacy. Ryker followed, taking me in.

"How are you doing with everything? I still can't believe Dex would go to this extreme."

"Whoever you thought your friend was, you were wrong. He's not that guy anymore if he ever was. I'm sorry, but you can't keep holding onto Obsidian as we knew him. For all we know, that wasn't even the real him. He's killed people. Innocent people. And I, for one, am tired of feeling guilty for his actions. So, how am I? I'm pissed, and I've never been more ready to take someone down. You said you'd hold him responsible. So, the question is, will you stand by me or just be in my way?"

Ryker watched me through my speech, my shoulders straightening with every word I said, a promise zipping through me to hold them. This had gone on too long, MKG and Dex needed to be stopped. And I hoped Ryker would be with me. But either way, I knew I had three men who would be.

His eyes held mine, and I saw the truth before he even said it.

"I'll stand by you, Fin. Always."

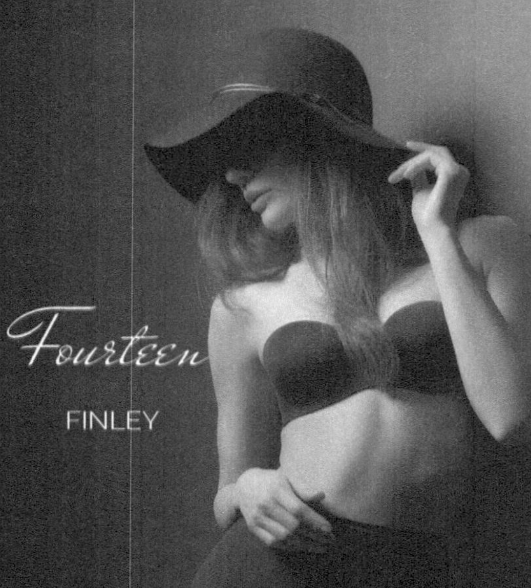

Fourteen

FINLEY

RYKER STOOD at the front of the conference table, a commanding look on his face as he debriefed everyone on what had occurred at the mall. The only thing keeping me from falling into a fit of hysterics from the ordeal was focusing on Dex and MKG. If they were this advanced, it would take the full force of The Order to deal with them, so I needed to focus.

"So, he was never there?" someone asked, drawing my attention as Ryker moved.

"No," he sighed, rubbing his hand over the top of his hair, the ends standing at all angles. "I don't know how far in advance he planned this or if he even had the capability of doing it so quickly, but there were five drones positioned around the mall, the majority of them in the food court area. The bomb was also placed in a shoe box display. He used a cell phone blocker to cut off communication. It was only our more advanced network with the watches that still worked."

Ryker placed his hands on the table, the weight of this visible as he glanced around the room at everyone. "There's something else."

I looked to Asa and Cohen, both shaking their heads that they didn't know. When I met Ryker's eyes, I knew it wouldn't be good.

"As I'd feared, Kristina has been killed by MKG. Her body was found at the mall. She's been dead for a few days. I've given her team a few days off, but I'm sure they'll want in on the takedown. Because there will be one. Dex won't get away with this."

Ryker's words were filled with truth, and I knew that even to his own detriment, he wouldn't rest until this had been dealt with. It had gone beyond duty at this point. It was personal, and Ryker didn't seem like the type of man to let something like that go. Dex had been his friend, and this was the ultimate betrayal.

"We have a team sweeping through the footage to see if they can find anything. I doubt there will be much, but no one is perfect. He's bound to have slipped up somewhere, and we'll be there to exploit it. Everyone else needs to train and work on their projects until we have more information. No one is to leave base unless it comes from me. As for now, only critical missions and agents already in the field will continue to operate until we have more of a handle on MKG. Dismissed."

Everyone began to gather their things to head off to do the tasks Ryker had set before them. I stayed sitting, wanting to talk to Ryker. I watched him, noticing how shaken up he was. The Order had been the thing whispered in the night for so long, restoring balance in the world one mission at a time, that now, to be the one being hunted was throwing them all off their game. I didn't think they knew how to act without their secrets and code names.

"Did you need something, little hacker?" he asked once the room was cleared, only I and my guys left.

"Yeah, I just wanted to make sure you were okay."

His brow furrowed, and I knew I'd taken him aback. He hadn't expected me to ask him how he was doing. I guess being the one in charge, he was used to always being asked for something. It made me want to check in with him more often.

"I'm..." he shook his head, dropping the act as

the lie fell away. He walked toward me, sitting on the table between Cohen and me. Despite the gruesome news, it felt normal for him to still flirt. At least, I thought this was Ryker flirting. "I'm trying to hold it together, but I feel like I'm failing at every corner," he said, his head dropping.

I swallowed, not knowing what exactly to say. "I don't think you're failing, Ryker. You're doing what you can to fix a problem. To stop a madman."

"But The Order is meant to stop these things before they happen. I can't help but feel responsible for the deaths in that mall, for the trauma you endured, for the scars Milo will have... it makes me wonder if someone else was in charge if they'd have caught it sooner. Did my friendship with Dex cloud my judgment of what he was involved with? How did I not see it coming?"

"Whoa, whoa, whoa. Okay, you can't go down that path, man. You're only going to drive yourself crazy," Cohen said, squeezing Ryker's leg. "And I think your history is what makes you the perfect person to be in charge because you know him the best. What did you always tell me? Hmm?"

Ryker turned his head, searing his eyes into Cohen's. If I ever questioned their chemistry, it was laid out right in front of me. It was magnetic, and I hoped they'd find a way back to whatever lay between them.

"Carrying the weight of the world around becomes burdensome and endless. There are plenty of things to genuinely feel guilt over in life, so you don't need to add to it by carrying someone else's. Instead, focus on what you can do to relieve the world of evil, redeeming your sins one mission at a time."

Cohen smiled at Ryker, and I let his words circle in my head. He wasn't wrong. I'd been carrying the sins of myself and others for years, and it hadn't brought me any closer to feeling redeemed. If anything, I'd felt guiltier each time I enjoyed something for myself. The lies I'd told myself had stained my soul like lipstick on a collar. I couldn't carry the weight of Dex's actions, killing those people to get to me, just as Ryker couldn't. I think I'd been focusing on everyone else to ignore the reality of the situation. But that wasn't going to help them or me.

I might not be responsible, but I could do something about it.

"Perhaps it was the hubris of The Order that blinded everyone to the threat brewing. It doesn't matter how he was able to amass power now; he already has it. What matters is what we do to stop him. Your friendship might have clouded your judgment, but I don't think it will any longer. You see him for who he is and what he's done. And I think that's what matters. We all have sins, Ryker. I ran from mine for so long that I thought the only way forward was revenge. I set out on a course with a plan to make you pay, and then I discovered that you weren't the monster I thought you were."

"Well, I might be a monster in other ways," he said, followed by a grimace. "Sorry, vulnerability is hard for me, and my go-to is either raucous sex jokes or guarded indifference. I'm trying to be present because you all matter. This matters. I don't want to lose you again."

Cautiously, I reached up and took his hand. His breath caught in a gasp at my touch, and I focused on looping my fingers with his. I felt Asa's hand on the small of my back, urging me on. Letting out a breath, I met his eyes.

"You won't lose me. Just be honest and no games. I can't take the lies anymore."

"I promise." Ryker turned his head, finding Cohen. "And you?"

Cohen looked over at me, and I nodded, letting him know I supported his decision. "I'm here too. We can discuss what that means after we handle MKG. Deal?"

"That's one conversation I look forward to having

for once." Ryker's face broke out in a genuine smile, and I felt a part of my heart I'd thought long lost begin to thump again. "Well, I have a few more meetings I need to have. Can we all do dinner later? Karen's been asking about you in the canteen."

"That sounds like a plan. It might be good to leave our suite for once. See you in a few hours then?"

"It's a date." Ryker winked, jumping off the table and sauntering to the door. The three of us stood slowly, following, and I wondered just what we were in for. Ryker Jenson was a mystery I was eager to uncover.

WHEN WE WALKED BACK into the suite, I found it filled with shopping bags. I stopped, blinked, and then blinked again when they didn't disappear.

"Okay, I'm not dreaming. So, why are there so many clothing bags in our suite?" I asked whoever knew the answer.

Milo limped out of the bedroom, startling a little when he saw us. "Oh, hey. I didn't hear you." He smiled sheepishly, and I knew, whatever the reason for all the bags, he was responsible.

"What's with all the bags?" I asked, walking closer to him. I instinctively placed my hand on his forehead, checking his temperature. He smiled down at me.

"I'm the doctor, remember?" He tugged me into his arms, and I carefully wrapped mine around him. "And I'm not broken. Still a little tired, which is why I didn't go to the meeting, but I promise, I'm good." He kissed my forehead, a soft smile spreading as he stepped back, his hands on my forearms. "As for the bags, well, I felt bad that all the things you'd picked out had gotten… misplaced. So, I took the opportunity to get replacements. I hope that was okay?"

I hadn't even thought about the clothes, which was a first for me. I guess I was worried they'd bring bad memories, but as I looked at the bags filled with untold treasures, the same feeling of euphoria began to crawl through my body at all the possibilities.

"More than okay. Oh, I can't wait to see what you got!" I clapped my hands as joy escaped through my body from my head to my toes. This was precisely what I needed. A good distraction from everything else.

I began to open bags, oohing and aahing at tops, skirts, pants, socks, bras, panties, and even shoes. Milo had thought of everything, and not only had he gotten me new things, but the guys as well.

"That doctor memory of yours must come in handy, remembering everyone's sizes," I said as I looked in awe at the display.

"As much as I would love to take credit for that, I called and asked the guys." Milo blushed, the red creeping up his neck, and I found it adorable. Walking over, I was careful of his injuries as I hugged him, pulling his face down for a kiss.

"You're adorable, and I love it. Thank you. You're going to spoil me, though, if you keep doing this."

"Nothing would make me happier, darling."

Fluttering my eyelashes, I fought my own blush as I peered back at the guys. "Does this mean I can style everyone tonight?" I rubbed my hands together in excitement.

"Sure," Asa said, sitting on the couch and picking up a bra. "This is my color."

"Not really your size, though. I think you're more of a 38 C, bro," Cohen teased, picking up a shirt. Asa laughed, sitting the bra back into the bag.

"Now this I like," Cohen said, looking over the shirt. It was blue and went perfectly with his eyes.

"Good, because I want you to wear it with these." I handed him gray pants, and he nodded, taking the things and walking to the bedroom.

I began to put the clothes in piles so they could

sort out their things, and I could get all of mine out of the living room. "Hope we have enough room in the closet," I groused, worried I'd have to pick and choose which to hang.

"Actually, we're being moved," Milo said, just as Cohen walked out, an odd look on his face.

"Is that why none of our stuff is in the bedroom?"

"Yes. I got the message after all this had been cleared through security. Ryker fears there's a mole in The Order. Someone had to tell Dex how to track our movements or where we'd be. So, he wants us in a more secure area. We're to get dressed and leave everything else, which will be moved while we're eating dinner."

"Wow, he could've mentioned it," I grumbled, feeling a little out of the loop. But knowing he had a million things on his mind, I wanted to give him the benefit of the doubt he would've at dinner. Packing up all the items, I left everything by the door that wasn't what I needed for us.

I handed a pile of clothes to Asa and Milo and then took my own into the bathroom. I jumped in the shower and rinsed off my body, managing to keep my hair out of the spray. Once I was done, I dressed in the new clothes, feeling all kinds of hot and badass in my sparkly shorts, slinky tank, blazer, and black high heels. Whoever said that clothes couldn't change the world clearly had never worn something this awesome.

When the guys took me in from head to toe, I could tell they also agreed with me.

WALKING into the canteen felt different this time. I knew these people and was one of them. That sense of belonging I'd always craved crashed down onto me, and my step faltered.

"Careful, little hacker," Ryker's dark and delicious voice cooed from my side, his palm resting on my elbow. "You look decadent."

As I looked at him, I tried to hide my blush, but it was a lost cause. Taking a few more steps into the place, I was yanked out of Ryker's arms as Karen pulled me into a hug. Her warmth and friendliness went a long way to cure some of the homesickness I'd been dealing with.

"It's so good to see you, Finley. I keep telling Cohen to bring you by more. I swear, he just wants to hog you for himself." She tutted at Cohen, who slung an arm around me, a broad grin on his face.

"Can you blame me, Karen? Fin's one of a kind." Karen stopped her huffing, smiling at Cohen with motherly love.

"Well, okay, I guess you're forgiven. I saved you the best spot in the place." She winked, walking us over to a large booth that was private but seemed to also have the perfect view of the whole canteen from the stage to the front door.

Asa and Milo sat on one end, and I scooted into the middle, wondering if Ryker or Cohen would be next to me. I didn't miss that they'd also be by one another. Asa squeezed my thigh, and I wondered if my boyfriend was up to some well-meaning matchmaking.

"I need to apologize about the room switch, Fin," Ryker said as he slid in next to me. "In the hustle of everything, it slipped my mind. It would ease my worries if all of you were better protected."

"Thank you. We appreciate your thoughtfulness," Asa said, speaking for the group. Before we could talk more about it, the server arrived and told us the specials for the evening.

"We have chicken Alfredo, broccoli Alfredo, or prime rib tonight. Who would like to start?"

Once our order was submitted, the server left, and silence fell around the table. Ryker cleared his throat, looking to Milo.

"How are you healing, Milo?"

"Pretty well. The technology and medical science you have here are outstanding."

Ryker smiled with pride, and I cataloged it away with the new information I was collecting about him. I liked that he was pleased with Milo's assessment, and I knew it meant Ryker worked hard to make The Order better under his command, even if no one knew it was directly him responsible.

Which, in and of itself, was a huge thing. Most people wouldn't be okay without taking the credit or being publicly recognized. I realized the brilliance of The Order for hiding people's identities. Not only did it provide a level of safety and keep the playing field equal among peers, but it kept away anyone who was only in it for the glory. It was hard to be power hungry when no one knew who was in control.

"So, Ryker," I started, then realized I'd blurted into a conversation. "Um, sorry. I was thinking and then thought of something I wanted to ask and didn't check to see if anyone was talking. Wow, self-absorbed should be my middle name."

The guys chuckled, and Ryker nudged me, gaining my attention. "You're the furthest thing from self-absorbed, little hacker. Maybe a little lost in your own thoughts at times, but I'd never think it was because you were only focused on yourself. So, what did you want to ask me?"

His eyes twinkled, and I decided I wanted to make them do that more. It was lovely and completely changed his whole face. In fact, I was a little lost in them as my brain seemed to lose all reasoning.

"Oh, right," I said when I realized I'd been staring. Licking my lips, I glanced around the table, finding all the guys watching me. It was a heady moment to find the four hottest guys I'd ever met all staring at me. "I honestly can't remember," I said after a minute, and nothing floated to the top. "I think I was going to ask you what your plans were after you retired. Yeah, let's go with that."

He chuckled, his face adoring as he gazed at me. "You know, until recently, I hadn't the slightest idea. I kept hoping for inspiration to strike me. But honestly, I figured I'd end up as one of those guys who couldn't stop working and stayed beyond his prime. A sad sack who everyone felt sorry for, but no one was willing to say anything to my face."

Ryker shrugged his shoulders, and something in me pinged in sympathy. I knew that feeling, where you didn't know which direction to go, but staying felt like you were only going through the motions, not really living. I didn't want that for anyone. Clearing my throat, I held his eyes and asked him the next part.

"And now? You said up until recently."

"That I did." He smiled, swiveling his gaze between Cohen and me. "I'm learning that there's more to life than work and that when you have the right people in it, you don't need to try so hard to push them away."

"Finley has a way of making you see that you're not the product of all your failures," Milo said. I peered over at him, seeing the earnest truth in his eyes. "I worked so hard to be the opposite of my family, but I wasn't really doing anything about it. When I met Fin, I saw what that indecisiveness was doing to me and the world around me. I wasn't making it better by being different if I was letting them continue their evil plans. You're in good company to be with while you determine the next steps if you want it."

I was surprised by Milo's offer to Ryker. Not by what he'd said, but that he was opening himself up to Ryker. Part of me hadn't wanted to think about this life working, but the guys kept proving it to me every day in big and little ways. They showed me how serious they were, so I needed to start accepting them.

"Thanks, man," Ryker said, nodding at Milo. "For what it's worth, I think you've done more good than you give yourself credit. And I'm all for figuring out what life has to offer outside these walls. First, we need to capture Dex and shut down MKG. Then, I'll gladly take you up on your offer to figure things out together. That means a lot."

Our food arrived not long after, and we ate our meal, talking about random things, no more big speeches or vulnerability shared. It felt nice to just talk, laugh at jokes, and catch up on things outside of The Order. And even trying to explain how our relationship worked.

"So you mentioned your twin sister is dating Fin's brother and six other guys, and you're cool with it?" Ryker asked.

"Yeah. It sounds weird, but I've played hockey with most of those guys for years. I know them. They're good guys. But also, she was already establishing a relationship with them before we knew we were siblings. So, it wasn't really my place to come into that and say anything. They've created a family, and I know they all love each other. It works." Asa shrugged his shoulder, the movement rocking me since one of his arms was draped around me.

"Is that how you got the idea to date three guys?" Ryker asked me.

"Actually, no. I fought it for almost a year. It wasn't until I ran to find you that these two teamed up and talked." I gestured to Asa and Cohen. "Milo I kind of pulled along for the ride. The three of them have been part of my life for this past year, and I was only fooling myself with the connections we had. I didn't think I deserved for multiple men to love me with all the things we'd done with MKG."

"I'm sorry you thought you were responsible for Mongoose. I never wanted you to carry that. I wish I'd tried to find you sooner. With everything that happened after, my hurt feelings got shoved to the bottom, and I didn't look at them, too afraid to see what you might have meant to me since I was under the impression you'd bailed. I was a coward, and for that, I'm sorry."

"Thank you, I appreciate it, but if I'm not responsible for Mongoose, you can't take responsibility for my guilt either. Let's just promise to talk through things instead of assuming and running off scared this time. Deal?"

"Deal. That goes for you too, Cohen. I don't want to lose you even if all we ever become is friends."

"No running." Cohen nodded, and I could tell something was swirling in his mind. "Well, we better head to our new room so we can get settled."

"Yes, I'll, um, show you where."

We slid out of the booth and waved goodbye to a few people as we made our way to our new suite. It wasn't in the same hall as before, and I tried to remember how to get to it as we took a few turns.

"Um, so, we kind of share a unit," Ryker said, and I could've sworn he blushed.

"Oh, um. Okay." I lifted my shoulders and eyes to the guys, not knowing what it meant or what to do in this situation. The perfect Fin in me wanted to say it was cool, but I couldn't tell if it really was or if that was my knee-jerk response. Sometimes, it really sucked being a people-pleaser when you couldn't determine whether your reactions were legitimate or from years of kowtowing.

"You have a separate sleeping area. These units are more for families, so the bedrooms are on one side, and the shared space is a kitchen and living room. So, if you don't want to see me that often, you don't have to. These are just more secure, and I wanted you to be closer. Sorry if that was presumptuous."

"I mean, it was a little, but I don't think you have anything to apologize for. Thank you for considering our safety, Ryker. Do we get into these the same way?" I asked.

Ryker seemed to exhale in relief, his whole body unraveling as he nodded, one corner of his mouth lifting in a smile. "Yeah. Just place your hand. Other than us, only my security detail has access to these."

I placed my hand on the scanner, the familiar tingle warming my palm as it scanned me. When it beeped, I opened the door and stepped in. Immediately I was hit with Ryker's smell. It was a combination of coffee, eucalyptus, and rain. Not that I smelled him often. Nope. Not this girl.

The area was modern and designed beautifully. It had a personality, and I could tell it was his home rather than a standard room we'd been staying in. There were paintings on the walls and little hints of him around the space. It gave me new insight into the man, and I liked it. To the right were an oversized sectional couch, two armchairs, and a coffee table facing a fireplace with a flatscreen over it. To the left was an immaculate kitchen that appeared to have all the latest gadgets. The whole space was nice and not what I'd expected. The guys looked as impressed as I, looking around our new space.

Ryker cleared his throat, rubbing the back of his

head. "Your rooms are through here. There are three, though one of them has two beds in it. I didn't want to presume what your sleeping situation was. I put all of your belongings in the biggest bedroom, Fin. It had the largest closet and its own bathroom. There's another Jack-and-Jill bathroom between the other two rooms."

"And where's your room?" I asked, turning to look back at him. He pointed in the opposite direction.

"My suite and office are on this side. Both hallways have keypads, so you can lock your side of the suite off at night if you desire."

"I doubt that's necessary, but thank you for the option," Cohen said, taking charge of our group. "We should get ourselves settled. Tomorrow is a busy day. Thanks for dinner."

Ryker nodded, standing with his hands in his pockets as he watched us walk toward the other hallway.

"Help yourself to anything in the fridge, and if you find you're missing something, just let me know."

"Thanks, Ryker. Goodnight."

"Night, little hacker."

He smiled, relaxing some, and I waved as we

headed toward our corner of the world, knowing that my life would be different from this point forward. I could feel it in the air. A turning point was just around the bend. And for once, it didn't scare me.

FINLEY

WALKING DOWN THE HALL, I peered into the rooms. When I spotted a mountain of bags, I knew I'd found mine. The room was gorgeous, decorated in grays and blues, with a massive bed in the center. There was even a little vanity table and mirror off to one side, and as I stepped into the master closet, I squealed. The guys chuckled, moving on to theirs.

"Now, this is a closet."

Sighing with happiness, I began sorting my new clothes, hanging them up with care like the treasured items they were. The closet had shelves and slots for shoes, and I realized it was almost my dream closet. Once I had everything in its rightful place, I checked out the bathroom, practically squealing again.

"Okay, this place is amazing. I might never want to leave."

"Talking to yourself," Asa said, coming up behind me.

"Yes, and I don't even care. This place is incredible." He wrapped his arms around me, kissing my head.

"Yeah, it is. You should see the other rooms." Taking my hand, he pulled me down the hallway to the room he'd claimed with Cohen. It was nice for a guest room with two queen beds and a decent closet. It was decorated in gray and hunter green, making it a soothing and relaxing environment. Walking through the bathroom, I was impressed with the shower and dual sinks they had as well. I softly knocked on the other door, finding Milo in a gray and red room. He smiled as I walked in, placing a shirt on a hanger.

"Hey, do you need help?" I asked but then realized there weren't any more clothes on the bed.

"Nope, that was the last one."

"How are you feeling?" I asked, taking a seat on the corner of his bed.

"I'm good, darling. I promise."

"Well, the reasons I ask, I was wondering if you'd like to take a bath and spend the night with me tonight?"

"Oh." His cheeks began to redden. "I'd love that.

How about you get the tub ready, and I'll bring some clothes."

Nodding, I walked back through the bathroom, giving Cohen and Asa kisses goodnight before heading into my room. I stripped my clothes and walked into the bathroom. I'd spotted a bottle of bubble bath earlier and wanted to try out the jacuzzi tub. Turning on the water, I let it run as I squeezed some bubbles into it. Once it was halfway, I slid into the water, the warmth rolling over my skin in a caress. Pulling my knees up to my chest, I laid my head on them as I sat in the water, the sound of the tub filling lulling me into a place of relaxation.

"You look peaceful," Milo said. I turned my head, the smile I wore sliding off my face as I took him in. He was only in his boxers, and I licked my lips as I took him in. His muscles weren't as defined as the other guys, but I could see them in his arms and abs. Though it was the little patch of dark hair that trailed down into his boxers that had my attention.

"If you keep looking at me like that, I don't think the bath will last long," he purred.

Lifting my eyes to his, I winked. "Maybe that's my devious plan."

Chuckling, he slid off his boxers teasingly, pushing them down his legs, his cock falling forward once it was free. I blinked, not expecting it to be hooded. The longer I stared, the more it began to grow and peek out at me. It transfixed my eyes, and I kept staring as Milo walked toward the bath and stepped in. He slid behind me, and it was only when he was out of sight that I was able to blink again.

"I think you have a Medusa peen." I dipped my head back, catching his eyes.

"Oh? Because it's hypnotic, or you're afraid it will turn you into stone?"

"Definitely hypnotic. I hope it turns me into goo, not stone."

Milo laughed, the sound almost as hypnotic as his penis. I pulled his arms around me, his Medusa dick brushing against my back. I tried to ignore it and just enjoy being in his arms. We sat nestled together for a while, the warm water soothing my body as I ran my fingers up and down his arms, the bubbles leaving trails.

"I'm glad you feel like you belong with us," I said, tilting my head to look at him. "I ignored my heart for a while, but now that I'm letting it be open, I couldn't imagine my life without you. You give me comfort and peace, Milo. You make me feel needed and strong, but also like it's okay to not have it all together."

I turned, the water swishing as I straddled his lap, my arms going around his neck. My boobs were no longer concealed by the bubbles, and his eyes drifted down for a second, and I felt him swallow, his dick twitching beneath me.

"I was so scared when the explosion happened. It's hard to describe everything I felt during that attack. I'd been frightened when the gunshot went off, but then you reminded me I could do this. You took off, helping all those people, and I knew I wanted to be as brave as you. So, I pushed my fear aside and figured out a solution. You gave me the courage to do that. For a few moments, I felt so alive when I finally cracked the code, the feeling of adrenaline I chase pumped through me, and I couldn't wait to find you, to share in that victory," I said.

"You were brilliant, Fin. I was so proud of you."

I smoothed my hands over his face, partially because I could, but also because I still needed to reassure myself he was all in one piece.

"I thought this was the life I wanted. To be chasing that feeling and putting myself in danger. But watching you fly through the air was one of the worst moments of my life."

"I'm sorry, Fin. I..."

"Ssh, I'm making my big romantic monologue, and you're ruining it by being understanding."

Milo chuckled, his fingers sliding to my back. "Okay, carry on."

"I've learned so many things on this journey, but the biggest has been that once I stopped running from my past, I could see all the incredible things already in my life. Somewhere between fighting my feelings for you and you continuing to patiently rescue me, I fell in love with you. And when I thought MKG had taken you from me, I realized how stupid I'd been. I don't need to chase the high anymore because being with all of you is better than any puzzle I could solve."

"You love me?" he asked, his eyes soft and hopeful.

"More than words allow me to express."

Milo surged up, kissing me, taking over as he wrapped his arms around me and pulled me closer. Thoughts fled me as I gave in to the feeling of his tongue twirling with mine. The water moved around us, the sound competing with our pants and moans. His skin was slick, and I slid my hands over it, feeling all the curves and muscles his body held. I was careful of his wounds, making sure not to aggravate them. When my hands found their way back to his hair, he moaned, and I realized that Milo liked it when I tugged on it.

"Darling, if you keep doing that, I'm going to embarrass myself," he panted, breaking away from my mouth to peer down at me. "As much as I'm enjoying our bodies together in the water, I'd rather be able to cherish you from head to toe without the fear of drowning or falling on something. How about we end the bath and move to the bed?"

"You have the best ideas."

Laughing, I stood and stepped out of the tub as he pulled the plug, the water gurgling as it began to drain. Drying myself off, I kept my eyes peeled to his body as the water showed more of it to me. I was barely able to focus on the task at hand, so transfixed by him.

"You're going to make me blush if you keep looking at me like that," Milo said, standing as he took the other towel on the counter and began to dry himself. When his body was covered, it allowed me to blink and return to my task.

"Medusa dick," I muttered, shaking my head.

Milo laughed, and I tossed the towel onto the counter, standing naked before him. I did my power pose, placing my hands on my hips as I dared him to not become mesmerized by my naked body. He gulped, and I watched his throat bob with the action, a satisfied smirk spreading across my face.

"Come and get me," I teased. Spinning, I took off for the bedroom. I made it two feet out of the bathroom when arms wrapped around me, pulling me to their chest.

"Gotcha."

"No fair, long legs." I pretended to pout, but in reality, it felt nice to be held by him. He carried me to the bed, and I felt the hard flesh between his legs. I was becoming addicted to watching his twitching Medusa dick. I couldn't wait to feel him in me. The new experience was something I was eager to try.

Placing me gently on the bed, I wondered what kind of lover Milo would be. He seemed like the type to edge you all day and cherish your body until you wept for release.

"You're so beautiful, Finley," Milo breathed, taking my foot as he began to trail small kisses up my leg. "And I love all the little sounds you make, the way you smell and taste, and I love that you take things head-on, even if you don't believe you do. I see your strength, courage, and love for those around you. You might think that people only like you because of what you give them, but I see the truth, and the reality is that people want to be around you because of who you are. Not what you do for them. You're a beacon of light and love, bringing joy wherever you are, and it draws us all to you. I never imagined someone as beautiful as you are inside and out could ever see me. Now that you've said you love me, I'm never letting you go. I hope you realize what you've unleashed in me."

As Milo talked, he kissed his way up my body. I bucked and whimpered with each one, needing him to give me more.

"Good," I hissed. "Now I can call you my boyfriend."

Milo chuckled, taking my lips with his in another devouring kiss. Taking the opportunity, I wrapped my legs around his waist and drew him closer. I could feel the tip of his penis nudging at my center, and all I wanted was to pull him in.

"Milo, I need you," I whined, hopeful that he would take pity on me and give me what I wanted.

He pulled back, pushing my hair out of my face. "I had plans to bring you to three orgasms before I allowed myself entrance."

"While that sounds heavenly, can I get a raincheck? I want you in me more than anything else. Please, Milo. I'm begging."

"You should never have to beg, Fin. Do I need a condom?"

"No, I'm good."

"Me too."

"Then what are you waiting for?" I teased.

Milo pulled back, spreading my legs and peering down at my pussy. He licked his lips, and I worried he would go back on his decision. Thankfully, he stroked his cock before lining himself up to me. I felt him begin to push in, and I wanted to cry out in relief. I needed to be filled by him.

"More," I gasped, my hands clinging to the bedsheets as I arched my back.

Looping my legs into his arms, he drew closer and pressed further. It was hard to think about the other guys' dicks while he was in me, but it felt like Milo might be the thickest of them all. When he was finally all the way in, I moaned in relief. He panted, and I could tell he was holding himself back.

"Don't hold back. Wreck me."

Milo looked into my eyes for a second before pulling back and slamming into me. With my back arched off the bed, I felt every inch of him as he withdrew and plunged back in. The only thing I could grasp onto was the sheets, so I clenched them between my fingers so tight, I worried I'd ripped them. But I didn't care as I moaned, his cock hitting me in all the best ways.

His muscular thighs flexed beneath my butt cheeks, and I succumbed to the lust coursing through me as pleasure ran through my entire body. A tingle began to build in my stomach as he pushed in, and my limbs started to go numb as I tensed them so hard. Everything built around me, and all I could focus on was Milo as he thrust in and out, slamming into me over and over, wrecking me just like I'd wanted.

"Yes, Milo. So good. So so so so, good," I cooed, the words barely able to form on my tongue as I arched up into him.

"Fuck, darling, you feel better than I ever imagined. You're so tight and wet. I could do this all night."

"No, no, I need it deeper. Faster. I just need to let go," I cried, not knowing what words were.

"Yes, darling."

The feeling in my heart I got each time he said that about split me in two when he reared back and plunged so deep into me, I saw stars. The feeling I'd been chasing began to crest as he did it repeatedly, not letting up for a second as I mewed around him in nonsensical words.

When I couldn't take it any longer, I let go, the tightness in my gut erupting and flooding through my body as everything trembled before going lax. I felt Milo thrust into me a few more times before he stilled, falling to the bed beside me. I tapped him, my words slurring.

"That was... yeah..." Milo laughed as we lay there, both of us panting for breath.

"You said you loved me," I said once my heart rate appeared to be back to normal.

"I did. I love you, Fin."

"I love you, Milo."

Turning my head, I found his beautiful eyes peering at me, and I smiled. I never knew I could feel so much love for people, but these guys showed me I could beyond my wildest imagination.

After cleaning up, we curled into one another's arms, and I fell asleep feeling safe and secure, knowing that whatever tomorrow brought, I had love, which was the best feeling in the world.

IT HAD OFFICIALLY BEEN one month since Finley and her trio of boyfriends had arrived at The Order and into my heart. I'd thought I'd been living life, but in reality, I'd only been passing the time. It was sad to realize that the one thing you needed in your life had been right there, waiting for you to wake up and know it too.

A few days after the MKG attack, Finley, Milo, and Asa had graduated from The Order training program, along with twelve other initiates. It was one of our bigger groups to make it through, and I was proud that one of my last tasks before stepping down was to ensure the program's future. Despite all my failings and baggage, I believed in what we did here and was glad it would continue after I retired.

Now, to just capture Dex and I'd be able to sleep easier.

A tap at my office door had me looking up, and I forgot for a second where I was as I stared at the girl who'd turned my world upside down in the most splendid way.

"Hey," I said, the word getting half stuck in my throat. I kicked my legs off the desk as I scooted in. Fin smirked at me, watching my every move. "What can I do for you?" I asked when she didn't move.

Her smile grew wider as she stepped into the room, walking closer and swaying her hips. Her outfit was outrageous for The Order, but it worked for Fin, and it was something I was becoming to love about her style. I gathered my composure as she leaned on the desk.

"Whatcha doing?" she asked, a tease in her voice.

"Going through all the data again. I feel like I'm missing something."

"Well, I had an idea. I'm not sure if it's stupid or not, but I wanted to see if you'd come and look at it."

"Absolutely." I slid out from my desk, walking around to meet her. I placed my hand on the small of her back as we walked out together.

"How are you today? I didn't see you at breakfast or lunch," she asked, tilting her head to look at me.

"Sorry, I had a board meeting early this morning

to update everyone on the MKG project, and my yearly physical was done." I peered down at her, watching her face.

"Did the board have anything to add?" she asked as we stepped into the main living area. It was empty since everyone was working. I stopped, not wanting to say anything out in the hall. She paused with me, turning to look at me.

"The board is worried that if we don't find him soon, his next attack will be even more devastating. They did a psych eval on his character to try to determine his motives. Based on everything we know, it's more than likely he's a sociopath with an antisocial personality disorder. This means he's prone to strike out in a fit of rage, taking out hundreds of casualties if he's not caught soon. We got lucky at the mall, but I don't know if we'll be as lucky next time unless he either gets what he wants or we find and stop him. Both of those options seem pretty hopeless at the moment."

By the time I was done, I was holding her arms, our bodies close to one another. I hadn't even realized I'd grabbed onto Fin, but she was becoming the life-vest I didn't know I needed. Laying my forehead against hers, I breathed her in, calming from her smell.

"You smell good, little hacker."

She chuckled, moving her head so she could look at me. "You do too. I always try to figure it out. There's coffee, but there's this fresh smell that reminds me of the rainforest."

"Ah, yes, my shampoo probably and aftershave."

"Hmm, whatever the combo, I like it."

Chuckling, I took a chance and pulled her into my arms, hugging her. Over the past week, we'd been growing closer, and I'd initiated a few small acts of touch. I always felt sick to my stomach before I did them, worried it would be the time she pushed me away. I wasn't used to feeling insecure about someone I liked, but I guess that was the difference. When I let myself think about it, Finley and Cohen were people I cared for. It was more than just getting her into bed. I wanted to be in her life.

"What was it you had to show me?" I finally asked, taking a step back. Her eyes lit up, and she took my hand, dragging me the rest of the way out the door.

"Like I said, I think it might be something, but I'm not sure." She bit her lip, a tell I was finding she did when she was nervous or unsure of herself.

"I'm sure it's something. You're way smarter than you give yourself credit for." I caught her cheeks blushing and felt pride bloom in my chest. I wanted to do more of that.

We quickly made it down the intersecting hall-ways to the workroom. When we neared, she dropped my hand, not wanting any of her peers to know. I knew it was necessary, but I hated losing her touch. Walking through the door, a few people looked up and nodded in greeting as we entered. I walked with her over to her workstation. Cohen and Asa peered up when we approached.

"Ryker," Cohen said, his eyes trailing over me. "How did the meeting go?"

"Some developments, but nothing we didn't assume. I'll fill you in more later."

He nodded in understanding, focusing on Finley. "You tell him what you found?"

She shook her head. "No, not yet." I looked at her, nudging her arm when she didn't say anything.

"What is it, little hacker?"

She began biting her lip again, and the number of things I wanted to do to her for the abuse, rammed into me. I quickly sat, needing to hide the erection growing in my pants.

"I began to think about Obsidian and how he operated. The fact that he did it out in the open for so long made me think. Did he want you to know? Was he trying to get your attention? If he's a scorned lover, that makes his thinking easier for me to follow. So, I put together all the information you have on

MKG and Dex. Using an algorithm I created for Sariah, I tweaked it to look for any places it overlaps or connects to see if I could find a pattern. Once I have that, we could use the program to help us predict future behavior. I just need more information than I think is in the files."

"Wow, that's brilliant, Fin. What do you need?"

"Since you lived with him, what were his daily habits? Any brands of foods he liked? Did he take any medication? Routines? Things like that."

I placed my head in my hands, trying to think of any habits of Dex's that stood out. "He was obsessed with a certain energy drink. It wasn't name brand, so he'd buy it in bulk. The cans were always on the floor. It was… Bang Shock! Because I used to joke that it was the only way he got banged. Geez, I was an ass." I hung my head, scrubbing my hand over my stubble. I needed to shave.

"Anything else?" Fin asked, an excited look on her face as she typed in the new information.

"Hmm, he didn't get out much, but did like to go to raves at the local gay bar." I slapped the table when I realized something important. "He had an inhaler."

Cohen grinned widely, typing some information into the computer he was working on. "Jackpot.

Prescription for Dex Callahan for Albuterol from five years ago."

"Perfect, let me add it and scan all the pharmacies in our search and see if any of his known aliases pop up."

I held my breath, feeling like it would be too easy to find him this quickly, but also glad to have it over with if it was. Dex was a noose hanging around my neck I was ready to shed.

"I… I… I think I found him," Finley said, raising her head to look around at us. She hit a button, and her feed went up on the big screen. I walked up to it, taking in all the parameters. It was a perfect match for a 25-year-old male who liked energy drinks, clubbing, had a prescription for an inhaler, high-speed internet, bought a smartwatch recently, and had been at the mall.

"Holy shit, little hacker. You're a genius."

I turned back to her, the whole room looking at the screen. She tried to duck her head, but it was no use; everyone was already looking at her with big smiles.

"What do we do next?" she asked, looking around at everyone.

Logistics and protocol ran through my head, and I knew I wanted to be on the team who scouted. "First, we send a small convoy to check out the intel. If it pans out, we'll look over everything and create a plan of attack."

"I'm going with you," Fin said, but I shook my head.

"No, little hacker." I hated seeing her upset, but she didn't need to be on this one. "It's just recon. I want you to keep searching and figure out his routine. Your algorithm has gotten us the closest we've ever been. We need to ensure that it wasn't his plan to leak that information to us."

"I'll go," Cohen said, standing and giving me a look that brokered no arguments.

"Fine," I sighed, pulling out my phone. "I need to handle some things; let's meet on the top floor in thirty."

He agreed, kissing Fin goodbye before striding toward the door. I hesitated before I left the room, wanting to kiss Fin or say something, but when I saw all the eyes looking at me, I stopped and waved like a middle school dork before walking out the door. Cohen snickered at me, and I rolled my eyes, trying to hide my heating cheeks.

"You don't have to hide your feelings. I'm sure everyone in there knows you have the hots for Fin. You have a stupid look on your face whenever you're near her."

"I do not." I scowled at him, but I wasn't sure if I was trying to convince him or myself.

"Yeah, you do. And you know we're headed to the same room. We don't have to meet up on the first floor."

"Sorry, I'm so used to giving orders that I didn't think about it. Thank you for going with me, though."

"You nervous about seeing Dex?"

"No. He's hurt too many people, making me wonder if we were even friends. I think we might have been more in his eyes than my own. I feel stupid for not noticing his obsession or involvement, though. That's what really gets me. Especially when he tried to hurt Fin and Milo. I never would've forgiven myself if something had happened to them. Now, I have the chance to make sure he doesn't hurt anyone else. I'm worried I'll snap and just shoot him without going through the proper channels."

"I'll keep you in line."

"I know you will." I turned, taking in Cohen. He seemed more at ease around me and not as resistant, making me hope that there was a future between us.

"I need to grab some things from my office and change into something that doesn't scream security or tactical team, and let my team know."

Cohen looked at me, scanning me again, and I

definitely felt more heat in his eyes as they caressed every inch of me. He eventually looked at himself, taking in his dark jeans and hoodie.

"I mean, I wear this all the time, but I guess I can change. What look are we going for?"

"Casual bystander. Don't want to stand out, just blend."

"Got it. I'll meet you here in a few." He raised one eyebrow, daring me to say the first floor.

"Fine. Here."

He smiled, and it cracked something in me. I felt a piece of my obstinate asshole attitude float away, and I wondered what these two were doing to me. Though, I had to admit it wasn't a horrible effect. In fact, I felt happier than I had in a long while. So, maybe I needed to shed some of my asshole ways and embrace this new softer side.

Changing into a dark pair of jeans, navy shirt, and shoes, I walked into my office and opened my gun cabinet. I selected a small Glock 43 for my ankle holster and a Walther PPS for my shoulder one. I slid a GPS tracker into my shoe and carefully placed fake fingerprints on the pads of my fingers. The nanotech dissolved into my skin once it made contact, making me shiver. Taking one last precaution, I swallowed a pill that wouldn't activate until after 24hrs, allowing it to pass any inspection if we were to be caught. It would give our team a chance to find us if everything else failed.

Taking a burner phone from the stack, I placed it in my pocket. The last time I'd used it had been when I thought I was playing a game with Fin. While that hadn't turned out the way I'd expected, at least she was here now and safe. In fact, with her passing The Order training, she could handle herself out in the field even better now.

And as much as that thought worried me, I knew she was more than capable of protecting herself and others. I couldn't cage Fin. She needed to fly, and I wouldn't be the one to hold her down. Even if I initially wanted to steal her away and make her mine, I saw and understood how her relationship worked now, and it was something I wanted for myself.

Sending a brief message to the board on the new updates, I closed my computer and locked everything down. I headed back into the main area and found Cohen waiting for me. Together, we made our way up to the first floor. After a brief rundown to my detail of what was going on, I took the keys to one of the SUVs, and we began our journey down the mountain.

It was quiet most of the drive, the radio playing music softly in the background as I followed the GPS to the location. Fin's research showed that he'd purchased a building a few years back. It was the only property in his name, so we made a guess that he lived there. Considering he wasn't seen out in public too often, and there wasn't any traffic cam footage, he either wiped everything when he left or had everything brought to him.

Knowing Dex, it was probably both.

It only took a few hours to drive to the town the address was in. I hated the fact that he'd been so close this whole time. As we approached the address, Cohen turned off the radio as I came upon the road. I was hoping there would be other buildings nearby so we could watch from afar. But it seemed Dex had been more innovative than that. Much like The Order's base of operations, it was secluded with what looked like one road in and out. I passed it, turning off the GPS as she insisted I make a U-turn.

"What now?" Cohen asked, trying to look between the trees, but it was impossible. We'd need an aerial overview to get a good look, which wouldn't happen today.

"I guess we find a base of operations and hit up some of his frequent spots. See if there's a motel nearby."

I was berating myself for not planning more before we left, knowing my exuberance to catch Dex had led me to be a little reckless. Cohen pulled out his phone and began typing things in a search engine.

"There's one a few miles from here. I can call and see if they have a room?"

I nodded, but my eyes focused on the rearview mirror. We were still on a deserted road and hadn't passed any other vehicles in miles. So when the dark car pulled out behind us, I knew we'd been made.

"Shit. Hold on."

Cohen looked up as I took a sharp turn onto a dirt road, hoping the car wouldn't be able to follow. Speeding up, I pressed the accelerator to the floor, needing to gain some distance. Cohen held onto the door handle, casting me an anxious look.

"That him?"

"I think so. Hold on. I'm going to try to lose them."

Just as the words left my mouth, I crested over the top of a hill, catching some air with the speed I was traveling. Because of that, I realized too late that we'd fallen for the easiest ruse in the books. My obsession had led me to make careless mistakes, and now I was going to pay for it. The worst part was that Cohen, and subsequently Fin, would too.

The vehicle crashed down, and I barely had time to swerve the barricade as we careened off the dirt path, dodging trees as branches scraped the outside of the vehicle.

"Shit, shit," Cohen screamed, and inside I agreed with him, but none of my words seemed to want to come out, dying on my tongue.

As the SUV finally stopped, I knew it didn't matter. We would be surrounded within minutes. We'd willingly driven onto enemy territory and offered ourselves without a fight.

I'd laugh at how absurd it was if it hadn't been me.

The car clicked as the engine cooled, and I tried to think of a way out of this situation. But I knew it was pointless. I'd seen his compound as I crested that hill. Dex was prepared for everything, and there was no way out.

Turning my head, I took in Cohen's eyes, the storm brewing there had my heart skipping a beat, and I hated I had to be the one to say it to him.

"I'm sorry, Cohen. Fin was right. My own hubris has been my greatest downfall."

He didn't say anything. He didn't need to. I could see it written on his face. The car doors were yanked open a few seconds later as men surrounded us. With one last ditch of hope, I pressed the emergency button on my watch, praying it would get off a signal before everything was stripped from me.

Hands pulled me from the car, throwing me to the ground, their faces covered by black balaclavas. Holding my finger over the side, I kept it there until everything went black around me, glad that I'd made Fin stay back. At least now she'd be safe.

Eighteen

FINLEY

SOMETHING WASN'T RIGHT. I could feel it in my bones. It was an hour past when Cohen and Ryker should've checked in. It had been quiet at the base, and I was trying to chalk my anxiety up to nerves, but I had a bad feeling, and it wasn't going away.

"Anything?" Asa asked, setting some food next to where I'd holed up. I had three computers opened, trying to find out as much information as possible on Dex and MKG.

"No," I finally answered, looking up to catch his green eyes. "I'm worried."

"Hmm, well, training states that if someone hasn't reported in six hours past their time, activate the tracker in the car and then the chip."

"Why do I feel like six hours might be too long?

Am I being ridiculous? Is it just because it's Cohen and Ryker?"

"You're not being ridiculous. And yes, I think you're more worried because it's them, but it doesn't mean your fears are unfounded. Since both Ryker and Cohen are gone, both of our superiors are in the field, so I guess that makes you the de facto leader. So, team leader Finley, what do you want to do?"

His words shook me, but I realized I liked how they sounded. I kept thinking that I was the weaker of the group or lesser than when I had to stay back, but that wasn't the case. Before, I ran into danger without proper knowledge of what I was getting into. It was naive and completely what teenagers did. But it didn't mean I'd do that now.

In fact, I'd shown myself and the others I could be calm under pressure. I needed to quit putting myself in a box and kick those walls down and make my own way.

"You're right. I am the team leader." I sat up, my hands planted on the desk. "And that means trusting myself. I'm going to pull up the GPS on the vehicle. At least if I can get a visual, then I won't worry."

"Sounds like a plan, team leader. What do you need from me?" Asa asked, lifting his eyebrows when I looked up. Was it bad I found it sexy? Yes, I needed to focus. I could explore wanting to dominate Asa later.

"Can you get Milo and look through the blueprints I pulled up? We need to know what we're dealing with if they were taken."

"Absolutely. You know, you're sexy when you get all bossy. We can talk about whatever it was that flittered across your mind when everyone is back here safe and sound."

My cheeks heated, but I nodded, looking at the screen as I began to type in some credentials. When I didn't hit any walls, I was surprised to find that Ryker had given me full clearance. Well, hot donuts!

With ease, I located the vehicle they'd taken and picked up the bowl of noodles Asa had left me. I slurped them into my mouth as their route filled the screen. Based on the address, it all seemed standard until the end, when I noticed a sharp turn on an unnamed street. Clicking it, I maximized it as I began to study it more.

It was like this, with noodles half hanging out of my mouth, that Asa and Milo found me a few minutes later. They both laughed as I quickly slurped them down, wiping my chin as I zoomed in on the screen.

"I think I found something!" Their amusement

shifted to concern as they crowded behind my computer screen.

"What is it?" Asa asked, not understanding what I'd stopped on.

"Ryker took a sharp turn here and then appears to stop based on the jagged line here. Then, the car is turned around and taken to a motel."

"Okay, so they're at the motel?" Milo asked, stepping back and crossing his arms. His glasses sat on his nose today, and I smiled at him.

"No, I think that's what MKG wants us to think. They had to know we'd check the GPS route and wouldn't be concerned if they ended there. They didn't take into consideration that the one checking it is a hypervigilant girlfriend who notices the smallest details."

"Oh, so you're Ryker's girlfriend now?" Asa teased, nudging Milo.

"What? Huh? I mean…" My face grew redder the longer I tried to find an answer for them. Waving them off, I focused back on the screen, clicking on a satellite to see actual footage.

"Ah, so she didn't deny it. I think we have a new brother-husband, Asa," Milo said, leaning into his counterpart. He'd gotten more comfortable with the guys since we'd proclaimed our love for one another.

"I'm ignoring you."

I kept clicking on folders, amazed at how much access to top secret things The Order had.

"Whoa, is that satellite legal?"

"I dunno. I didn't stop to ask. I could use it, so I did. I figured it wouldn't let me if I wasn't supposed to." I shrugged my shoulders, entering the coordinates I needed. "Besides, I doubt MKG would allow a satellite to be over their property, so I'm going to have to be fast at accessing this."

Using the information from the route, the coordinates of where they turned, and the time of day they appeared to be there to filter, I was shocked when an image began to load a few minutes later.

"Wow, I hadn't expected it to work that quickly. Technology really is amazing."

"Tone down the love affair with tech. Look, can you zoom in there? It's hard to see with the trees, but it looks like…"

"Bodies being pulled from the vehicle," I said, barely a whisper. "Monkey balls."

My mind began to race with what I needed to do. Hitting print, I gathered as many pictures as I could before they were lost to me. When I tried to follow the truck they were loaded into, the whole screen went blank, and I lost the connection.

My heart was racing, my hands shaking as I tried

to focus on how to help them. Steps, steps, steps, I repeated, needing to remember them.

"Fin," Asa said, handing me a phone. "Call the security office."

"Right, okay, yes." I took the phone, typing in the number when I remembered we were supposed to keep this a secret in case of a mole. "Um, wait. Who was Ryker's guard today?"

Milo typed something into a laptop, pulling up a list of names. "Bishop, Anderson, and Sharpe."

"Nicole," I wheezed. "It couldn't be Nicole, right?" I knew it was a high probability that those three people were either the only people we could trust today or the three we couldn't. I just had to figure out where they fell on the line.

My head began to swim as dizziness took over. I didn't know if I could do this. Ryker and Cohen were in danger and depending on *me* to rescue them.

"I don't know what to do," I admitted, tears threatening to spill. "What if it's the wrong decision and I get them killed? I wouldn't be able to live with myself."

Hands gripped my face, and I stared into Asa's green eyes. "Fin. You're the best person for this. I believe in you. Milo believes in you. Ryker and Cohen believe in you so much that they left you in charge. Stop stressing about what could happen and focus on saving them. Don't let fear rule you. You're brilliant, Fin. Let your genius out to play. You said you wanted to trust yourself; this is your chance."

"You make me sound like a superhero." I smiled, sucking in a breath. "Okay, you're right." I was Finley Amelia Reyes, and I was a badass. Time to woman up and remember that.

Taking a few calming breaths, I quit worrying about not making it to them and focused on finding them instead. This was a puzzle I could solve.

"Okay, look into every communication and routine of the three on Ryker today so we can know if they're clear or our targets."

"On it," Milo said, taking over one of the laptops open on the table next to us. I looked to Asa, scanning through my head what we needed to do next.

"Contact Samson and see if there are any guys he trusts in the area. They might be able to get there before we can, and we know they won't be turned."

"That's smart. I'll make the call." Asa walked to the front of the room as he dialed his biological father, and I returned to the computer. I needed information about their headquarters. It was safe to say that if they were taken, we'd been right about their location.

My phone buzzed, and I jolted back in alarm at the name until I remembered this was Dex's MO.

Cohen: We're here. Ryker's being annoying as usual. Nothing to report. Will probably head home tomorrow. Miss you.

My hand hovered over the phone as I debated what to type back. Finally, I knew I needed to play along.

Me: Bummer. Hopefully, you can get some sleep. Miss you too.

It was kind of lame sounding, but I didn't know what else to put without giving it away that I knew it was Dex. At least I could identify what was real and not, and that wasn't anywhere close to how Cohen talked. An idea began to build, and I ran over to Milo. He peered over at me as he scrolled through messages.

I reached over to him, selecting the three people's phones we were monitoring, and just as I expected, a message from Ryker came through.

Ryker: All clear. Will return tomorrow.

"Did all three receive that?" I asked.

Milo shook his head before clearing his throat. "No, Bishop didn't receive it."

"Bishop… so he must be our traitor—MKG's inside man."

A pit of despair wanted to swallow me whole at the implication. Bishop was Cohen's friend and had worked at The Order for years with Ryker. He was in his mid-thirties and, from what I gathered, was considered to be upper-management for The Order. It made sense how he had as much information as he did, but it also saddened me. Shaking off my melancholy, I focused on what I needed to do.

"Okay, we can use this. We need to gather a few people we can trust without alerting Bishop until we're ready for him to leak information."

"Got it. I'll work on it while you and Asa find us a way into the compound."

Kissing his forehead, I walked up front to the smart screen that had the blueprint on it. After a few seconds, I realized I didn't know what I was doing. It was all just a bunch of blue lines to me.

"Yeah, I can't read this. Who can we get to help with this?" I asked, looking at Asa. He hung up the phone, joining me.

"Samson has a few people he trusts he will send to scout out the location. I told them the information we knew so far, so they'll be discrete and see if they can get a drone to fly over to get the layout." He turned, taking in the blueprint. "As for this, Bishop is the best at deciphering them."

Grimacing, I shook my head. "Anyone else?"

"What did I miss?"

"I believe he's the mole. Texts were sent to me and to Sharpe and Anderson, but not Bishop, leaving me to believe he's the traitor. He wouldn't need a reassurance text because he knows they've been captured."

"Hmm, well then maybe Caleb or Asher. I can go and get them without causing a scene."

"Thanks. We must keep what we're doing quiet for as long as we can. It might be our only advantage."

Asa nodded before heading out the door, and I went back to my computer. I needed to develop the best tactical plan in the history of strategies and know what security measure I'd be up against. Knowing Dex, it would be a lot.

Cracking my knuckles, I zeroed in on my task, pushing the fear and insecurity away and zoning in on my boss bitch energy. It was time to rumble.

Nineteen

COHEN

SHARP PAIN RADIATED THROUGH ME, and I grimaced as I tried to move. Everything hurt, and I struggled to remember why. We'd been driving and talking when we'd had to take a sharp curve… the chase, collision, and capture ran through my head at top speed, leaving me with a wince.

"Fuck, that hurts," I wheezed.

A grunt of pain sounded next to me, and I sucked in a breath as I turned my head. Something dripped down my face, obscuring my view. My hands were tied behind me, so I couldn't move to wipe it out. Blinking, I tried to keep it out of my eyes as I took in what I could. We were in a medical room. Which wasn't what I'd expected at all. White walls, stainless steel, and a white tiled floor surrounded me.

The sound was a little louder this time, and I recognized it. "Ryker, can you hear me? You awake?"

"Mmm, barely," he said, his voice pained.

"My memory is fuzzy, but I think we were captured?"

Ryker snorted, but even that sounded painful. "Yeah. Sorry, I got you into this mess."

"I'm pretty sure I volunteered," I said, my lungs beginning to hurt. "Any clue how long it's been?"

I didn't want to think about Finley, too scared I'd never get to see her again, which, of course, meant she was the only thing I seemed to be able to concentrate on. The part of my brain that was working also knew that she might be the one thing that kept me pushing through the pain to survive.

"What do we do now?" I asked Ryker, who wheezed a little laugh.

"Not sure," he said. "I haven't even seen Dex yet. It's just been goons giving us these blows."

"Is he mad, or is he wanting something?" I asked.

"With Dex, I never know."

Almost like he could hear us, which, knowing how tech savvy he was, he probably could, he walked through the door a moment later.

"Gentlemen," he said, spreading his arms in greeting with a smug smile.

The effort it took to lift my head to glare at him

was excruciating. I wanted to sneer back, but the muscles on my face refused to obey. I blinked, trying to get the blood out of my vision to see him clearer. I tried to catalog all the features of the man in front of me. He was only moderately tall, probably around 5'10". He had mousy brown hair, a strong jawline, and wore a suit. Outside of his attire, nothing stood out about his features. Though, it was his eyes that scared me. They were hollow, no ounce of humanity in their depths.

"What do you want?" Ryker asked.

"To punish you, of course." I didn't miss the manic sound in his voice as he said it or the way his eyes shifted back and forth, always falling on Ryker. It was clear the dude was obsessed with him.

"Fine, take me. Let him go," Ryker said.

"But what's the fun in that?" Dex responded, clapping his hands. "He needs to be punished. You care for him; therefore, he's valuable to me."

"I'll do whatever you want. Just let him go."

The psychopath walked forward, gripping Ryker's face between his hands. Blood poured over his fingertips, but he didn't seem to care. In fact, if I saw his eyes correctly, his pupils were dilated; he was enjoying it.

"Oh, baby. I have so much in store for you. Don't be giving in to me already. It takes out all the fun when you don't scream." Dex squeezed Ryker's cheeks before planting a kiss, and my whole body tightened as a feeling of possessiveness surged up.

I growled, pulling at my bindings, but they were too tight and my body too sore.

"Now, let's have some fun, shall we?" Dex asked as he grabbed a scalpel off the medical kit lying to the side. Faster than I could blink, he stabbed it into Ryker's leg, a shout leaving the man I knew I loved but had been too afraid to admit.

"No!" I screamed as Ryker bent over, his face pale. The chair moved only a millimeter, and I knew there was nothing I could do. This was beyond torture, having to watch someone you cared about be hurt while you sat back helplessly.

Tears I didn't know I was crying fell down my cheeks, mixing with the blood, blinding me even more. I'd never wished for something to turn back time as much as I was in this moment. I couldn't even decide where it had all gone wrong. Should we have not come back to The Order? Or was it just coming here to scout with Ryker, who had been too reckless and impulsive? I'd give anything to know what the right decision was.

Since I couldn't turn back time and wasn't a fortune teller, I focused on what I could do now in the situation. My options were pretty limited, considering I was tied to a chair. But I had training. I'd practiced; surely, I could find a way out of this. I focused on my wrist bindings, twisting them a little to see if there was any give. They were tight, meaning I wouldn't be able to Hulk my way out of them.

Instead, I would need to do the most painful approach. Did I have time? Or was this my only moment?

Looking over at Dex, I wished I hadn't, considering I caught him with his hand down his pants as he stroked himself off looking at Ryker's bloody body. The leer on his face said it all.

"Just you wait, Ryker baby. I'm gonna make it really good for you." He started to unzip his pants, and I squeezed my eyes shut, not wanting that image in my head.

When a beeping sounded, he cursed, and the fiddling of pants stopped. I peeked open my eyes when it sounded like he was on his phone, assuming it was safe.

"What?" he screamed. "Take care of it," he said. "No, I'm busy."

It didn't seem like the person on the other end of the phone was agreeable. Dex let out some expletives, cursing them, before tossing his phone across the room.

He turned back to Ryker, continuing to ignore me

as his cock peeked out of his unzipped pants. I squeezed my eyes shut, but the image was already there.

"I'll be back, baby. I have to go take care of something. I'm the boss, after all. No one knows how to do shit without me. I'll show these assholes how to do their job without their thumb up their asses. Maybe I'll give you some pain meds if you're good."

He stroked Ryker's bloody face, not at all bothered by the blood on his hands. I heard him zip up his pants before he strode out of the room without a backward glance. My shoulders sagged in relief before I tensed. This could all be a trap, and he was watching us, but I had to take it for what it was. A free moment.

Sucking in a deep breath, I braced myself for what I had to do next. Hopefully, I was in enough pain already that I wouldn't notice it. Pressing my thumb against the chair leg, I moved it back and forth until I heard the snap. My eyes watered and I grimaced. But I couldn't focus on it. With my thumb out of the way, my wrist could slip through the binding, and I pulled my arm forward.

My shoulder hurt from being yanked back, and it took a moment for me to get any feeling in my fingers. I cradled my hand against my chest, but I knew I had to move. Standing, I wobbled with the chair until I could grab something off the medical kit so I could cut my other binding. Once I was clear of the contraption, I picked up the phone to see if it still worked. I knew it was risky using his own technology. But knowing a few backdoors, I hoped to get around it so I could get a message sent out.

Logging into one, I made my way over to Ryker and cut his binds. Scanning his injuries, I grabbed a first aid kit and worked to bandage the most severe wounds.

He mumbled groans as I worked, but didn't resist. Once I had him patched up, I went back to the phone to see if I could get a hold of Finley.

ME: Sweetheart, use this IP to find us. I'm
trying to break us out. Send help. I love you.

It wasn't the most romantic thing, but it was concise and all the time I had for. Erasing my footprint, I tossed the phone back where I'd found it and grabbed a few things from the room we could use for weapons. Who was I kidding? That I could use. Ryker was in no shape to fight.

Lifting him up, I placed one arm around my shoulder as we began the slow process to the door. He was already panting when we made it there, and I was sweating from the exertion myself.

"Just leave me. Get help and come back. If I don't make it, tell Finley I regret not kissing her just once," he whispered, most of his words barely coherent.

I wrestled in my brain with what to do. I didn't want to leave him, but I also knew he was right in that there was no way we'd make it any distance with his condition. But if I left him, I might never see him again. I might never have the opportunity to tell him…

"I…" the words died on my lips. Gulping, I wetted them as I stared into his eyes. "I'll come back for you. I promise."

I pressed a gentle kiss to his lips before very carefully setting him down on the ground by the door. I handed him a weapon so he might be able to catch whoever entered by surprise and save himself some pain. Ryker squeezed my hand and took a breath as I gripped the doorknob.

Turning it, I waited for an alarm, half expecting guards to swarm the area the second I stepped out. The hallway was oddly quiet and devoid of anyone, but I didn't take that to mean I was safe. Creeping along the wall, I tightened my hand around the knife I'd grabbed. The blood was no longer in my eyes, but the pain still throbbed through my body with each step. I didn't think I'd ever get the feel of their fists out of my head.

An elevator dinged ahead, so I quickly ducked into the first room that didn't have a keypad on the door. Shutting it quietly, I stayed hidden in the dark, praying the footsteps would keep moving.

"The boss has lost his marbles," a voice said, coming closer to the door. "First, he had us kidnap these two dudes and then beat the crap out of them. Now that we have an actual breach in our system, he doesn't even seem to care. I joined MKG because I wanted to show the world I was smarter than they thought."

"Pfft," another guy chuckled. "I joined to get rich."

"Yeah, okay," the first guy agreed. "There was some of that too. But this is beyond either of those. It feels more like a terrorist group than hackers quietly taking money out from under the rich's noses."

"For sure. That whole mall thing was insane. It still gives me nightmares thinking about that. I couldn't believe he had us plant those drones and then stay to watch. He's sick, man."

"Yeah, well, it's not like we can defect. You saw what he did to all those others who wanted to leave. We're down to half our numbers as it is."

The more I listened, the more hope bloomed that maybe we could make it out of here if MKG wasn't at total capacity. An idea began to form, and I knew it would be risky, but it might be the only way to make it out alive and back to Finley.

Taking a deep breath, I gripped the doorknob and opened the door. Both guys turned, guns lifted at the sound. I raised my hands, not even pretending to be a threat.

"Looks like we have a runner," one of them said, but I focused on the other, the one who'd been talking about the nightmares.

"I think we could help one another. The Order is onto MKG, and it's only a matter of time before they storm this facility and take over. Once that happens, your chances of not rotting in a prison cell are slim. I'd like to propose a trade."

The one guard scoffed, turning to look at his friend. He had a contemplative look, and I knew I had him.

"What's your trade?" he asked. His friend rolled his eyes, but the one who'd been haunted held mine.

Smiling, I laid out the deal, hoping to ensure our safety and give Finley and The Order enough time to arrive.

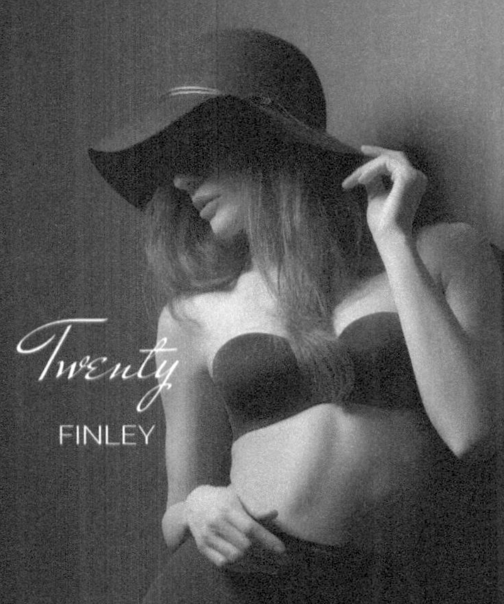

Twenty

FINLEY

ANXIETY COURSED THROUGH ME, making my palms sweaty and my heart race, but I was here and confident about my plan, so I wasn't going to freak out now. Asa and Milo had helped me perfect it, and I trusted our judgment and plan to get our guys back. I believed in us… and me. It was a whole new feeling, and I wrapped it around me, helping to stop some of the trembling.

"You got this," Asa said through the comms, somehow knowing I'd be fretting. Smiling, I centered myself as I stepped out of the car and began my walk up to the building. I was decked out in leather pants, knee-high stiletto boots, and a red leather jacket. I'd taken my look six years ago and ramped it up, aligning it with who I was today. I'd never felt more like the femme fatale than I did right at this moment. Using that energy, I strode forward.

"I know this isn't the time, but damn, Fin, you look so hot right now. Go kick some ass, and try not to give Cohen and Ryker a heart attack when they see you," Asa said, making my nether regions heat.

A giggle escaped me at his insinuation, letting the rest of the nervous tension leave my body. Just because I was walking into a building that housed a psycho killer didn't mean I had to be scared.

Balderdash! Why did I have to think of it that way?

Before I could fret too much, the door opened, and a man I'd never met, yet who had caused me so much torment, stepped out.

"Can I help you? This is private property."

"Oh? Is it? I couldn't tell with all the signs and creepy boobie traps that you didn't want guests." It seemed my brat filter was activated when I was crapping my pants.

The man regarded me, barely holding a sneer back as he took me in from head to toe, playing dumb like he didn't know me, and I wondered how far he would take that. "If you don't leave in five seconds, I'm calling the police."

He crossed his arms, and I caught a streak of blood across his knuckles at the action. My heart raced faster, but I focused on his eyes. His dead, soulless eyes.

"Oh, yes, please do call the police. It will save me a phone call."

"Pardon?" he scoffed, clearly not amused with my witty banter. Too bad, I was hilarious.

"The cops. You said you would call them if I didn't leave in five seconds. Well, it's been fifteen seconds at least, so please, call them. I'll wait." I crossed my arms this time, pretending to be the one who was impatient and mocking him all in the same move.

Our plan was simple. I needed to keep Dex occupied and away from Cohen and Ryker long enough that the team could extract them with limited casualties. It was just the getting away part myself I was still unclear on. Hopefully, before that occurred, the actual government would be here with Samson's connections.

"I don't know who you think you are, but I'm done." He went to close the door, and I tutted, shaking my finger at him.

"Now, now, Dex. That's no way to greet an old friend. We were friends, weren't we at one time? Or was it all a play from the beginning?"

His face morphed from one of disinterest to calculating as his whole posture changed. "Well, Finley, I guess if you know who I am, then there's no need for us to beat around the bush. I was trying to be charitable since I already have who I want, but if you insist on annoying me, I can add you to my torture list. I do like to play with my things."

His face twisted, and a cold chill ran down my back. This wasn't a man that could be fooled or who'd go down easily. Dex was truly a psychopath who knew no bounds. He'd take what he wanted, not caring who or what he destroyed on his path to get there. My limbs became frozen as I held his eyes, not wanting to appear weak. But I was. I so was.

I was the prey here. There was no doubt about it.

"So, why don't you come in and tell me all the little stories you've concocted about me to make yourself feel better? I do find them so entertaining. I always loved manipulating you into believing Ryker liked you. You were so gullible, believing anything I told you." He paused, his eyes traveling up and down me. "It seems you still are naive. Your lipstick can't cover all the lies you tell yourself."

Dread filled me as my heart raced. I hadn't anticipated the mental battle he'd wage. He tilted his head, almost like he was listening to something, before a creepy smile spread across his face freezing me on the inside.

"Oh goody, it seems whatever backup you were

expecting has been, how shall I say it, um, yes, *bombarded.*" Dex threw his head back, cackling like he was the world's funniest comedian. He rubbed his hands together, that smile spreading across his face sending fear cascading through my body.

"Do not step into that building, Fin!" Milo shouted into my ear, and I winced, causing Dex to smile even wider.

"Your team telling you to retreat? How about we strike a deal? Want to play a game, little hacker?"

"Don't call me that," I said, anger burning the fear away. "You might have been able to pretend to be Ryker online, but you'd never pass in person, and you know it. You're not even a quarter of the man he is."

"Ah, it seems like someone's crush has come back full force. Too bad you won't get to have your happy ending. The only person who gets one here is me." He reached out, attempting to grab me, but I blocked it and knocked his hand away with one arm while holding the knife I'd slid into the hidden holster on the side of my pants. I palmed it, keeping it secret, ready to strike.

"Ooh, I guess the little hacker's gone through training now. That just makes this more fun."

He came at me from the opposite direction in a quick grab, but I ducked, sweeping out with my leg and making contact with his thigh, but I'd aimed too high and almost toppled over. I arched up with the knife, catching part of his arm as he grabbed my ponytail. I had a second to prepare for the sharp pain as he yanked me back. I tried to remember my training despite my thoughts screaming at me to get away.

A whimper left me as he began to drag me, and I kicked out, trying to catch the doorway with my feet. I swung back with the knife, making contact again, but it wasn't enough. My other hand went to his as I tried to pull it away. I didn't think in my panic, all my training and thoughts of escaping leaving me, only trying to disengage him from me. When I remembered I still had the knife in my other hand, I reared up, praying I wouldn't stab myself in the head.

When he screamed, I felt victory, pulling the knife free before he took my weapon. He didn't let go of my hair, so I swung up again, but he was prepared this time and blocked it, knocking the blade free of my hand. Tears stung the back of my eyes at the loss of my knife, and I scrambled, trying to pull free with both hands. I couldn't let him take me anywhere. I'd never see the light of day again if he succeeded.

Digging in with my nails, I threw down my weight and locked my hands around his forearm.

Twisting, I pushed forward and got my knees under me, giving myself more leverage. My scalp cried out, but it was better than letting him get any further into the building with me as his captive. I wasn't sure if he was lying about the backup or not, so I didn't want to be stupid and go any further if I could help it.

"Stupid bitch," he screamed. I knew I only had a few seconds before he acted out in anger and just slit my throat. Dropping my hands from his forearm, I heard him chuckle, thinking he'd won. Falling back on my butt, I caught him off balance as I kicked my feet up and nailed him in the groin with my pointy heels.

Dex doubled over, finally letting go of my hair. Quickly, I climbed to my feet just as he sliced out at me with my knife. It caught the back of my leg, and I felt the sting of pain as I kept moving. I couldn't focus on it. I had to get to safety.

The question was… which way was that? He'd gotten me further into the building than I'd realized. My comm had fallen out at some point, so I tapped my watch, hoping the guys were still there. I kept moving, too afraid to go back toward psycho-douche.

"Asa? Milo?" I squeaked, my voice not wanting to work. My throat felt raw, and I wondered if I'd been screaming and not even realizing it.

"Fin!" someone shouted. It was too hard to hear on the tiny speaker on my wrist who it was. "Fuck, babe, you scared us. Are you okay?"

"Um, I don't know." I glanced back, sighing a little when I didn't see anyone following me. I'd taken too many turns to know where I was. "I got away, but now I'm lost in his building."

"Shit, okay. I'll use your watch's location and blueprints to see where you are."

I took another turn, hearing a door shut, so I ducked into a room, looking for a window or something. "Someone was coming, so I'm in a room," I whispered. There was one window, but there was no way of opening it that I could see. It was one solid pane of glass. "I need to hide or find another way out," I said, looking around the room in a panic.

There were boxes in a corner, but otherwise, it was mostly empty. There were no real places to hide. I looked for a closet or any vents in the ceiling, but it didn't seem like I was that lucky. Moving over to the boxes, I opened one, curious about what could be in them.

"No, freaking way," I breathed, staring at the cans of gas. The next box had a gas mask, so I pulled it out, hoping they weren't a hoax. But what were the odds that I'd end up in this room? No, these were to be used at some point by MKG, and I just happened to get to them first. Grabbing as many as possible, I secured the mask and walked to the door.

"I'm heading out. Let me know when you have an exit route. Any word on the others?" I asked.

"Silence on that end. Just get out, Fin. We can make a new plan together. But if you're taken too, there's nothing for them to hope for, and I don't know what Asa and I would do," Milo said.

"Okay. I promise. I won't be a hero."

Opening the door, I peeked out, checking for anyone, but it was once again vacant. This place freaked me out, and I was ready to get out of there.

"If you go to your left, there should be an exit door if he hasn't remodeled or blocked it."

Sucking in a breath, I blew it out, forgetting about the mask. It fogged up as I took a step, and I cursed myself. Keeping my breath even, I took a few more steps, using my ears to listen while I waited to see.

"Hey! You're not supposed to be here."

I froze, then remembered the cans in my arms. Pulling the ring from the top, I turned and rolled the can before sprinting in the opposite direction. I didn't know what this gas did, but I knew it couldn't be good. I couldn't think about the effects it might have, or I wouldn't be able to go through with it. It might be foolish, but for the moment, I had to see everyone here as the enemy, or I'd never get out of here alive.

"You're coming up to it," the voice said, barely audible above my heartbeat pounding in my ears.

My heels clicked against the floor, and I once again wished I'd chosen different footwear. No one who wore stilettos expected to be running for their life.

"Turn to your right."

Following the command, I felt the elation begin to course through me at being so close to freedom. So when I smacked into a chest, I wasn't expecting it. The cans dropped from my arms, and I stood, frozen. Arms circled around me, pulling me to a chest, and I deflated, knowing this was it. I'd lost. I only had one move left, the last can held tightly in my grasp. Looking up, I met the eyes of my captor just as I tugged the ring free.

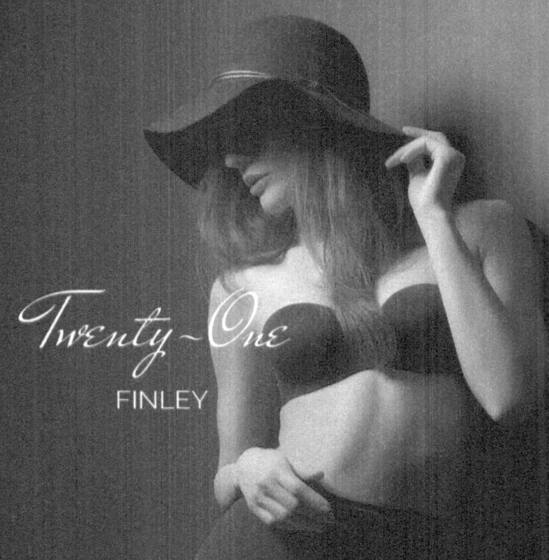

Twenty-One

FINLEY

SAMSON'S HAND clamped down on the pin, taking it from my hand. He held it steady before meeting my eyes.

"How you doing, kiddo?" He smiled, and my whole body sagged with relief. I wanted to weep joyfully, but I knew this wasn't the time. I pulled the mask from my face, pushing it onto my head so I could speak to him.

"I'm so glad to see you. When he said the backup had been intercepted, I got worried," I whispered, moving toward the door I'd been running toward. Samson followed, shoving his hand out the door and throwing the canister before closing it quickly.

He braced against the door, and I grimaced, realizing he thought it was a bomb. "Um, sorry, I think it's just knock-out gas."

"Oh, yeah, I knew that." Samson straightened, and I wanted to giggle, the emotion feeling nice after fearing for my life. The realization sobered me, and I remembered I was still in danger.

"So, what's the plan?" I asked.

Samson looked down at me, and I could tell he wanted to yell at me to run to safety, and yeah, that had been my plan mere seconds ago, but now that there was backup, it felt foolish to run away. I was trained and ready for this. I steeled my spine, giving him my no-nonsense look. If he thought his daughter was sassy, wait until he realized where she learned it from.

The look seemed to work when he exhaled, resigning himself to including me. "Apologies, Fin, but when I look at you, I see the best friend to my daughter, the girlfriend to my son, the little girl who used to design costumes for every stuffed animal in her house. It's taking me some time to remember that you've been through The Order training and are capable of handling yourself."

He blew out a breath, looking upward for something. When he returned to me, he no longer looked at me like the little girl he knew from the shadows, but as a colleague. It bolstered my own confidence, and I puffed out my chest.

"All the entrances are covered by our men. The

issue is that the team picked up explosives laced within the walls. If Dex feels like it, he could blow the building at any second. Most of the personnel and MKG guards have been apprehended. Some have been more than helpful in providing us with good intel on how to defuse the bombs, along with where Dex is more than likely hiding. The heat signatures only counted seven people before I entered, so we have to assume that there are at least three guards outside of Dex to contend with."

I nodded, cycling all the information through my brain. "He's going to fortify himself so that he can watch everything like he did at the mall. He's not one for confrontation, especially after I—who he considers the weaker sex—humiliated him by taking him down."

"That's what I'm thinking too. I studied the program you made. Stellar work. I'd like to talk to you about designing something for Alpha, but we can discuss that once we're out of here."

My face heated, and I nodded, pleased he'd liked my tech. "So, what are we doing?"

"I'm going to the control room to find the panel to defuse the bomb. You have to decide if you want to go after Dex or the guys."

I debated for half a second, but it was no contest for me in the end. I needed my guys back. I'd trust the rest of the team to take care of Dex. Even though it was tempting to kick his butt and slice off his penis so he couldn't use it again.

"The guys," I said when I remembered Samson couldn't read minds.

He nodded, handing me a gun and pointing toward a hallway. "They're on the bottom floor. There were two other body signatures with them, so assume they're guards. You won't be able to access the system without the right biometrics, so you'll have to climb down the elevator shaft."

Swallowing, I nodded, understanding the task. "Good luck, Samson. Thanks for coming."

"Always, honey. You're family." He gave me a quick kiss on the forehead before sprinting in the opposite direction he'd pointed for me. It took me a second to recalibrate myself to the fact that Agent Buttface had just kissed me on the forehead, but it seemed once he'd found his family and been reunited with the love of his life, he wasn't such a butthole anymore. Which was good for me since he'd be my father-in-law one day.

Shit. I wanted to marry Asa.

"Fin? You there?" I heard my watch say, and I wondered if Asa had heard me think that.

"Um, yeah. So, change of plans. I'm going after the guys, and your dad is going to defuse a bomb.

How badass is he?" I asked, peering around the corner before I sprinted. There was still one guard unaccounted for, so I couldn't be too careless.

"Did you just say my dad was badass? I don't know if I should be jealous or impressed you actually cussed."

"Hey, I cuss. I just use it sparingly so that you know it's important when I do," I huffed, running toward the next hallway.

I could hear Milo and Asa laughing, and I knew they were helping me focus by giving me something else to concentrate on.

"You're clear. No other heat signatures on the first floor. Samson has moved into position on the third floor," Milo said, and I raced toward the elevator.

Stepping into it, I peered up at the ceiling and instantly knew I couldn't reach it. Running back onto the floor, I found a chair behind a desk and picked it up. Returning to the elevator with the chair in tow, I positioned it under the hatch. Looking at my boots, I knew there was no way I'd be able to make it with them on, so with a regretful sigh, I pulled them off and shoved the last can of gas into them before tossing them out of the elevator. Maybe I could pick them up later? They were designer, after all.

Balancing myself on the chair, I slid the hatch open and managed to lift myself up into it using the arms. It began to wobble, but thankfully, I'd worked on my core and arm strength the past few weeks with training. Otherwise, I'd be stuck down there trying to find a rope or something while everyone around me died. Morbid thoughts there, Fin. I could never let Asa know that I was thankful for sweating or he'd never let me live it down.

Taking a second to catch my breath, I stood up and peered around the shaft. I almost wept for joy when I saw the little ladder on the wall. Walking to it, I was happy to find it was clear of the elevator, so I wouldn't get smushed if it started. It would be terrifying to climb down it, but I'd be out of harm's way for the most part. At least, that was what I told myself as I descended down to the lower floor.

Landing on my feet, I stood in front of the elevator doors and hoped they were easier to pry open than I imagined them to be. Pushing them apart with my fingers, I cried out when my nail broke, the doors barely budging. Cheese on toast!

Glancing around, I needed to find something to give me leverage. When I spotted a toolbox and a crowbar sitting against the wall, I welled up with tears at the discovery. Grabbing them, I pried the crowbar between the two doors, and using all of my weight, I pushed against the bar, crying out in joy when they opened enough for me to wedge between them.

Climbing out, I laid on the floor for a few seconds while I caught my breath. Holy pajamas, this spy stuff was hard work. No wonder everyone was so buff.

When my breathing returned to normal, I sat up and glanced around. I could only see a hallway, but it gave me a creepy vibe, and I dreaded having to go down it. Rising up, I began to stalk down it on my padded feet, remembering there were two other people down here with my guys. When I was a few doors down, I could hear talking.

Pausing to listen, I stayed still as I tried to hear what they were saying.

"We should just go. Something isn't right. It's been too quiet," a voice said.

"Boss wouldn't leave us."

"You sure about that? Okay, new plan, you have the key; let's get out of here and see what's going on," Cohen said.

His voice bolted me around the corner, not thinking about the danger, as I stepped into the light with my gun raised.

"You're not going anywhere without me," I said, tears falling down my cheek.

The four guys stopped, and that's when I realized that while there might be two guards down here, they didn't seem to be against Ryker and Cohen if the four of them sitting together and talking was anything to go on.

My eyes raked over both Cohen and Ryker, taking in every cut and bruise. Ryker looked the worse for wear, and I wanted to run to him and tell him how I felt, but it didn't seem like the right time with the bomb still a possibility.

"Sweetheart," Cohen said, moving toward me. The guards relaxed when they saw I wasn't a threat. Cohen wrapped me in his arms, and I held onto him, too afraid to let go just yet, the gun still in my grip.

"You're okay," I said.

"That's debatable. If you're down here, what's going on? Where are your shoes, and what's on your head?" He held me at arm's length, then noticing the gun in my hand, he took it.

"Let's move and talk. Ryker?" I asked, peeking around Cohen.

He opened one eye, and it felt like he was happy to see me. "Hey, little hacker. Looks like you get to save the day."

Rushing toward him, my hands hovered over his body, unsure where to touch him. Everything looked like it hurt.

"Now I wish I'd gone to Dex so I could cut off his penis and shove it down his throat," I muttered.

Ryker snorted, then grimaced, and I looked to the two guards. "I'm assuming you're *not* on Dex's side?"

They shook their heads, though one appeared doubtful, but I'd let it go for now if they helped us get off this floor. There was no way we would make it up the elevator shaft otherwise. Taking my power pose, I pointed at them both as I started to give out orders.

"Okay, then prove it. Carry him. We need to go. This building is wired with explosives, and we need to get out."

That had the guys moving, and Cohen took my hand as we started down the hallway. He leaned down, whispering. "Bossy Fin is super hot. You need to use that voice in the bedroom."

My cheeks heated, but I kept moving. No time to give into temptation until we were clear of danger. If I wanted to use that voice, I needed to make sure we were out of this alive.

We made it to the elevator, and one of the guards scanned their cards to call it. When it arrived without any issue, I began to relax a little. The five of us climbed in and rode it up, quiet as it ascended. My toe tapped against the floor, worried we'd get stuck in here.

The doors opened, and my gut sank as we spotted Dex waiting for us. He had Samson on his knees in front of him, a gun held to his head. Fear ran up my throat, and I tried to think of a way out of this mess. Dex smiled maniacally, and I wondered how he could have gotten the advantage on Samson. When I met Samson's eyes, he nodded slightly toward the mask still perched on my head. Remembering the can I'd thrown into my boot, I dropped my eyes to it, hoping Dex thought I was just scared.

"Well, well, well. Now that we're all here, who wants to die first?" Dex cackled like it was the world's funniest joke.

"How about you?" he asked and, a second later, shot the guard holding Ryker up. I screamed, not having expected the violence for some reason. The man fell, Ryker struggling to stay upright now that the man was bleeding from his chest. The other guard looked at Dex like he didn't even know the man.

Which let's be fair… he probably didn't. Not the real version.

My hands began to shake, my nerves over-whelming me. I couldn't think under this pressure. I needed to focus my attention, or I'd lose it, and we'd all die. I couldn't let us all die! I'd haunt myself in death, filled with guilt for taking all these people from the ones they loved—including myself.

Samson. I needed to focus on him. He seemed like the one with a plan. Glancing back at him, I noticed he'd been able to use the gunshot to his advantage, the canister now in his grip. He implored me with his eyes to pull the mask down. So, while Dex continued monologuing about how we were all such disappointments, I shoved the mask over my head just as Samson pulled the ring. The gas began to fill the space, and he lifted it up so Dex would get the majority.

I almost felt bad for Dex, the look of confusion on his face when his limbs began to grow weak. I just had to hope this was knock-out gas and not something lethal. Fudge, why did I have to go and put that in my brain?

The instant he dropped, I reacted, bolting toward him and taking his gun. I held it, my hands shaking, and I debated. He deserved to die, but could I be the one to do it? Would it be better to let him go to jail? Was that enough justice for the crimes he'd committed?

When a hand wrapped around mine, I saw Ryker standing there, his shirt over his mouth, keeping what was left of the gas out. He implored me with his one good eye to give him the gun. Without hesitation, I let go, turning my back as I bent down to help Cohen lift Samson up. He'd passed out too, being so close. We'd only taken two steps when the gun's pop sounded. I tensed, my step faltering, but I didn't stop. I kept walking, wanting to leave that place and never look back. I already knew it would haunt me for the rest of my life.

Stepping out the door, I practically wept as Milo grabbed me, pulling me into his arms. Asa took over with Cohen to drag his father to a nearby medic. I peeked over Milo's shoulder as he carried me, needing to see Ryker emerge. When I spotted the uninjured guard carrying him out, my body relaxed, the tension easing out of my bones.

"We did it," I said, then realized I still had on the gas mask. Milo lifted it up, peering down at me with love.

"I've never been so scared, darling. But you were amazing."

The tears I'd been holding back spilled over, and I clung to Milo as he carried me to the medic. It was done. My revenge had been finalized. The man who'd stolen my innocence was dead. I didn't feel like I'd imagined I would, and I knew it was because it had been my own guilt that had weighed me down all those years. Now that I knew that Mongoose was alive and Dex had been the one behind it all, I could let go of it.

I might have started this journey off for the wrong reason, but I was ending it for the right ones. I'd learned so much about myself and opened my heart up to, I daresay, four men. Now, I had my whole life to live with them.

STEPPING INTO THE ROOM, the first thing I heard was the steady rhythm of a heartbeat. The sounds of medical equipment beeping were becoming too familiar to me. Asa smiled at me when I approached, and I eagerly went to him, needing to feel his arms around me.

"Hey, kiddo," Samson said, drawing my attention to the bed. "You did good." He smiled at me, and I returned it, happy to have his respect.

"What happened after you left me?" I asked, taking in the cast and bandage. He gave a dark chuckle.

"I was able to incapacitate the other guard and make it into the control room. With the assistance of one of my hackers, I disabled the bombs and was looking for you on camera when I was attacked from behind. You were right, by the way. Dex had a hidden area in the control room that he'd been in. We scuffled for a little, but I was easier to subdue with a broken arm and stab wound than I'd like to admit."

I picked up his good hand, squeezing it. "You saved us. That's all that matters."

"Yeah, well, I wasn't sure what to do when I saw you all. Your mask gave me the idea when I saw the canister. I knew even if the others inhaled it, that at least you'd be able to get out. It was my last ditch effort to save everyone."

"Always got to be the hero," a familiar voice said as she entered the room.

"Sawyer!" Jumping up from Asa, I ran a few feet to my pint-sized best friend and wrapped my arms around her. She held me tight, and I didn't stop the tears that fell. There was nothing like a hug from your best friend to heal whatever you were suffering from.

"Wow, I can't believe she gets the greeting and not your own flesh and blood," my brother said from behind her. Rolling my eyes, I dropped Sawyer's arms and hugged my brother next.

"Hey, big Brother," I said as he wrapped me in his familiar Henry scent. His hug was longer and tighter than usual, and I wondered for the first time if I'd worried him.

"Hey, little Sis. I'm glad you're okay." Henry kissed my hair before stepping back, and I found Sawyer hugging Asa and her dad, griping at Samson for getting injured. Isla smiled over at me as she stood by her husband's side, holding his hand, smiling at their children.

When it was apparent we wouldn't get any more details from Samson, I excused myself from his room and went down the hall to check on Ryker and Cohen. They were being moved back to The Order once they were stable, but with the severity of Ryker's injuries, they'd opted to bring them here first since it was closer.

Knocking softly, I stood at the door and looked at the two of them. Cohen's smile immediately captured my heart, and he stood from the bed, already bandaged and dressed in some clean clothes. He tugged on my hand, pulling me into the room.

"Perfect timing, sweetheart. Please tell Ryker he's being a stubborn ass."

"You're being a stubborn ass," I said, not hesitating.

Ryker sputtered, looking at me in shock. Cohen cheesed, kissing me quickly before giving Ryker a smug smirk.

"What? You don't even know what about," Ryker argued, trying to shift but grimacing when something pulled at his injuries.

Jumping up on the bed Cohen had just vacated, I swung my feet as I stared at him. I shrugged one shoulder, looking at him.

"Don't need to. I know you, and you're always a stubborn ass. So, if Co-bear says you're one, then I believe him."

I heard Cohen groan behind me, but I kept my eyes locked on Ryker. His face stayed frozen for a second before he let out a laugh, then winced.

"Sorry, I'll try to keep my hilarity to a minimum." I jumped off the bed, tentatively sitting on the edge of his, and took his hand. "Ryker, what will it take for you to kiss me?" I dropped my head, the blush rushing up to cover my cheeks. But I figured we almost died. Why were we dancing around the issue?

He sputtered again, sounding like a drowning cat this time, so I braved it and peered up at him from under my eyelashes. His one eye stared at me, and I'd say I'd rendered the flirt speechless.

"You want me to kiss you? Even after everything that's happened? I thought—"

I lifted my fingers and pressed them to his lips. "Stop thinking. That's the problem." Leaning forward, I kept my eyes open, watching if he wanted me to stop. When I was only a hair away, I paused. "Too much crap has gone down to worry about niceties. I like you. Cohen likes you. I think you like us both. So, stop fighting it and sacrificing yourself for the greater good and just—"

This time it was Ryker who shut me up, pressing his lips to mine. My eyes stayed open, staring into his, and I saw the fear but also the relief and joy. Closing mine, I gently placed my hands on his jaw, cupping it as I pressed my lips harder into his. After a few seconds, I pulled back, giving him a lingering look.

"It was as perfect as I always imagined kissing you would be," Ryker whispered, lifting his one good hand to stroke my cheek and hair. "Even bruised, broken, and stitched up, I couldn't imagine a more perfect first kiss with you, little hacker."

"Now, will you agree to come back with us?" Cohen asked. He leaned into my back, and I suddenly realized how close he'd moved toward me. I dropped one of my hands and took his.

"That's what you're being stubborn over?" I rolled my eyes, giving Ryker a "see, I knew Cohen was right" look.

"Hey," Milo said, stepping into the room. "Everything is final with the real estate company. The house we wanted is ours." Milo grinned at me, looking at the other two men. "I'm glad you made it out, Ryker."

"Thanks, man. House?" he asked, looking at Cohen and me.

"Milo and Cohen are both stupid rich, so I decided to use that for my own personal gain for once. The rest of us will be returning to Utah, and you're coming with us. Lux has state-of-the-art physical therapy programs, and Milo will be the physician overseeing your care. We haven't gotten the opportunity to build our relationship the way I want…" Cohen cleared his throat, and I smiled. "Sorry, the way *we* want, and we both knew if, given the opportunity, you'd stay behind, siting something to do with recovery and overseeing the transferring of titles and blah, blah." I waved my hand, smiling. "So to circumvent all that, we made it impossible for you to say no. Besides, you deserve some happiness, and I want you around."

"Me too. Even though you annoy me at times, I can't deny the feelings I had for you are still there. The situation we're all in is unique, but I know if you stay back, you'll only grow further away from us, resigned to never be happy and just live for the job. I know you, Ryker. This is your chance to catch up, to get to know Fin and me, and see if this type of relationship works for you. You don't have to stay forever, just give us a few months and see where it takes you."

Ryker looked between the three of us, taking in our expressions. "You really mean all of that?"

"Yes, Ry." I smiled, squeezing his hand, and he softened.

"Okay, I'd like the chance to see how this type of relationship works. I already know what you all have is unique and special, and it would be a privilege to get a chance to find that for myself as well."

"Yes!" I jumped up, kissing his lips briefly before hugging both Milo and Cohen. "You know, despite almost dying… Nope." I shook my head, resetting my thoughts. "Actually, I don't want to qualify anything Dex did as fun. I'm glad it's over. I'm relieved we're all relatively unscathed, and I'm thrilled we've somehow all found each other through it. Yep, let's go with that."

The guys gave me soft smiles, and I knew that we'd all be okay despite our rocky beginning.

A WEEK LATER, we'd officially packed up our suite, most of it consisting of clothes and Ryker's belongings since we'd all only come with a few suitcases. After a few days to recover, we spent the rest in meetings and debriefings, talking about the incident and how to make sure something similar didn't happen again. Bishop admitted to being blackmailed and was brought up on charges of assisting a terrorist. It sounded harsh, but people wouldn't have died if he hadn't given our location at the mall, not to mention Kristina.

What impressed me was how The Order used everything as a teaching moment. It was weird being discussed openly without people knowing it was you in the room. But it allowed the other agents to see what had been done well and what could've been done differently.

"I liked how Agent Oblivion thought to use an outside agency, but I also think there was a way to utilize more of The Order's agents without arousing the mole," someone said, and I tried my hardest to keep my face blank.

It was an odd experience to sit through hours of strategic planning on something you'd done. I was glad that we'd be inactive agents after this. Ryker had bargained for us all to remain as part of The Order, but where we could go back and live our lives, only taking on missions when it fit our skills. It seemed like the best of both worlds for me. I'd get to be back with my family and friends, living a life I loved, but also have opportunities to live a little dangerously every now and then. It made my adrenaline junkie heart happy.

"Well, that's all for today. Thank you all for your commitment to going over these files. There's a celebration in the canteen for our comrades who will be leaving the base to return to their homestead," the instructor said, dismissing everyone.

I looked at the guys, smiling as we gathered our stuff for the last time. Cohen slung his arm around my shoulder, and I grabbed Milo's hand as Asa walked behind us, talking with Ryker. Despite Ryker's claims of being on the outside, since the attack, he'd loosened up and let the guys into his life. It made me happy to see our family unit bonding.

"So, hot stuff," Cohen said, grinning down at me, "what do you have planned for the rest of your life?"

"Hmm," I said, tapping my lip with a finger. "Well, naturally I want to start my own fashion label for ice skating costumes. The ones Sawyer sent me for Nationals were atrocious. The kids desperately need my wisdom at Lux, or they'll majorly screw up their social media presence. But other than that, kicking some bad guy's butts every now and then doesn't sound half bad. Why? What do you have in mind?"

Cohen grinned, bending down to whisper in my ear. "Oh, I plan to have you every which way and then back again for the rest of my life. What do you say, sweetheart?"

I gulped, nodding enthusiastically. "Yep. I'm good with that plan."

Milo chuckled next to me, and I glanced over, squeezing his hand. "I'm good as long as you guys are there. I don't care how cheesy or loved up that makes me."

"You could never be too cheesy, Fin. It's one of my favorite things about you. Plus, I had your fantasy closet built, so I'm not going anywhere."

"You did what?" I asked, stopping and making Asa and Ryker almost collide with us.

"I didn't expect Milo to spill the beans first," Ryker said, nudging him. Milo's face was red, but he shrugged.

"I couldn't keep it to myself any longer."

"You're serious? You built me my dream closet? I think I might faint."

"Wait until after the party. We have a long night of traveling ahead of us. You can faint when we get to the house. Deal?"

Jumping up and down, I kissed each of the guys

before tugging them into the canteen, even more eager now to leave. I'd come to The Order to settle a debt, and I was leaving with more than I could've imagined. Now, if I could only learn to not wear stilettos on missions, my life would be complete.

Who was I kidding? Fashion always trumped necessity.

A WEEK LATER

UNPACKING the last box of things from my room on campus, I didn't hear my attacker when they jumped on me from behind. The person was small, barely moving me, but I took a step forward to balance. Her arms wrapped around me, her pomegranate scent washing over me.

"Oof, you didn't stick the landing. Gotta mark a point off for that," she teased before hopping down and flopping onto the nearest surface, which happened to be a humongous bed.

"Hey, Sawyer," I said, smiling at my best friend. "Did you guys just get back?"

She sat up, smiling at me as she pulled her feet up under her. Sawyer began to survey the room. "Yep. It was nice to meet Mateo's family, but I'm glad to be back here. Though, I wish school wasn't starting in a week. Madeline has us training practically every minute of the day to maximize our time before the ice is overcome with students. I'm starting to regret my dream of going to the Olympics."

"No, you're not." I tossed a pillow at her head, and she caught it, a massive smile on her face. "You love to train."

"Yeah, you're right. It just feels weird not to complain about it. So I put on a good show for you."

"Haha. I'll have you know that I can now run five miles without getting out of breath." And shoot a gun, but I decided to keep that tidbit to myself. Didn't need to freak out my bestie.

"Wow, I'm impressed. Does that mean you'll sign up to do the charity 5k with us? Is there a Team FinSin in your future? Gonna take on team Bosh?"

"Ha! No, I said I could run it, not that I liked to. And we don't have a cutesy name. There's only five of us, so I dunno." I shrugged my shoulder, my face turning bright red, so I moved over to a different box to hide it.

"Shrug your shoulder all you want, Fin. I know you. What's up?" A pillow hit me in the side of the head, and I gave up my pretense of hiding and went and joined her on the bed.

"When we first left the base, I couldn't wait to all be under one roof. To have time to develop my relationships and become a family like you have with your guys."

"But?" she asked, nudging me.

"Now that the guys are here, I worry they'll regret it. Especially Ryker. Asa is still coaching, and Milo is doing his residency, so it's easier for me to believe they have other reasons to be at Lux outside of me. Cohen is always moving around, so him working for Samson also doesn't seem as such a big stretch. But Ryker…" I trailed off, ducking my head as I began to play with the bedspread.

"I don't know him as well as the others, obviously, but I know you, Fin, and you're amazing. I get it, though. There's a certain level of doubt that starts to creep in when you have more than one boyfriend, but I can tell you from experience that it's a wasted emotion. Trust them to know what they want and don't devalue their actions. But most of all, know your worth, girl. You're a brilliant hacker who can sew, knows fashion, and looks killer in a pair of heels. You're one of a kind, Finley Amelia Reyes."

"God, I've missed you." I tackled my best friend to the bed as we hugged and giggled. Cuddling together, I thought about what she said. "Thank you. I needed to remind myself. Now," I said, sitting up, "tell me all about Mateo's family, Ollie going to culinary school, and the new hockey coach. I feel like I'm so out of the loop."

Sawyer chuckled but sat up and filled me in on how things had been on campus over the summer and how she'd finally convinced Ollie to stop taking classes on the weekend and to just go for it.

"Dimitri was happy for Ollie and asked his help in finding a replacement since the Senior level needed a head coach and new assistant with only Fletcher staying on. Ollie and Dimitri talked about promoting Jacob, but in the end, they decided some new blood was needed to get the program back to where it was before the whole Council debacle."

"Why didn't they promote Tyler?"

"Tyler wanted to stay on the Junior team so he could still have time to work with Samson and his dad."

"That was Asa's reasoning, too," I mused, remembering Asa debating what to do. "So, who did they pick? Anyone good?"

Sawyer rubbed her hands together in glee. "Well, I'd like to think my influence has made Ollie a better man because he picked Henley Henshaw to be the new head coach."

"Wait, but Henley's a girl..." I trailed off as a smile spread across my face.

"Exactly. What better way to make some waves than to shake everything up? I think it's brilliant, and I'm really proud of them for being open to the idea."

"I'm actually excited about attending some games now. Who's the other new coach?"

She shrugged her shoulder, bumping mine. "I can't remember his name, Reed something."

"Doesn't ring a bell. I'll get the scoop from Asa later."

A knock at the door had us breaking apart and glancing toward it. Ryker stood there, looking a little awkward with Sawyer here.

"Oh, hi. You must be Sawyer. I'm so glad Finley found you." He stepped into the room, his hand outstretched toward Sawyer.

She hopped off the bed and met him halfway. "It's nice to meet you, Ryker. Thanks for saving my girl's butt a few times. Speaking of butts… I should go and find my boyfriends and head home. Ollie and Tyler were hanging with my brother."

She skipped back over to me, giving me a hug and kiss on the cheek. "Be good and remember your worth." Sawyer lifted her eyebrows, wiggling them as she gave us finger guns as she left the room.

"She's a character," Ryker said, and I laughed.

"That she is. How are you feeling? How was your physio today with Dax?"

"It went well. Asa, and I think his name was Rhett, joined me. Big dude, scary eyebrows?"

"That sounds like Rhett." I chuckled, walking closer to him. When I reached him, I wrapped my arms around his waist, resting my head against his chest. Things had developed more between us in the week we'd been here, but I could sense how he always waited for me to make the first move. I wondered if he was still worried I blamed him for Dex's destruction. After a second, his hands fell to my back, and I let out a contented sigh.

"I still have to pinch myself sometimes when you come to me so easily. I was wondering if you'd like to go on a date with Cohen and me?"

"I'd love to," I said, pulling my head back to see his face. He smiled, and I was glad he was holding onto me, or I might've wobbled as my legs grew weak. Ryker Jenson smiling was a dangerous weapon. "When are we leaving, and what should I wear?"

"In about an hour, and dress however you want. I love your style."

He kissed me then, our tongues twisting together as we fell into an easy rhythm. Despite only being intimate with one another for about a week, it came naturally. It probably stemmed from years of knowing him. Ryker was part of me, even if I'd never wanted to admit it.

Pulling apart, we were both breathless as we stood, staring affectionately at one another. Ryker's mouth curled up on the side, and he stepped back.

"Right, I'll leave you to it. I'm afraid if I don't that things will progress more, and we'll never make it to the date."

"I'm starting to regret the date if it means no fun time." I pouted, sticking my lip out as my hands went to my hips.

"Never said there wouldn't be any fun time, little hacker." He backed out of the room with a wink, leaving me hot and bothered.

Remembering he said I could wear whatever I wanted, I quickly ran to my favorite room in the house, letting out a blissful sigh as I took in the closet. It was the size of my childhood bedroom, with more walls than I had clothes. Sadly, the same couldn't be said about shoes as they filled in the little slots designed for them. In the middle sat a colossal island with drawers on every side that held all my underthings, pajamas, and anything I didn't want to hang up.

The far back wall had a three-sided mirror in the middle, a vanity filled with makeup and hair care products to the left, and my own design studio on the right. My beloved sewing machine sat next to a mannequin and a wall that was fitted with rolls of fabric, buttons, and anything I could think of adding to an ensemble. From the plush carpet, the attached full bathroom, to all my favorite things in one place, it was a miracle I ever left this closet. The guys had done well spoiling me.

Taking my time getting ready, I pampered myself as I went full Finley. I hadn't gotten this dressed up in a while, and I missed it. For the most part, there weren't many places to go in Oak Crest, and I spent the majority of my time hanging out. So, if we were going on a date, I would make good use of the opportunity.

Dressed in a black fly-away skirt with a white blouse that hung to my mid-section, red lipstick, and red heels Ryker had gotten me, to replace the deceptive ones, I finally felt ready as I took myself in from all angles in the mirror. A wolf whistle broke my concentration, and I spotted Cohen leaning against the island.

"Fuck, sweetheart, you look amazing. I can't wait to show you off and let all these other dudes know you're mine."

"Hmm, is that so?" I walked toward him, taking in his dark jeans and button-down shirt. Running my hands up his front, I ran the tip of my nails over his neck, and he let out a soft moan. The tiny hairs tickled my palms as I flattened them against his head.

Cohen's eyes were hooded as he stared down at me. "On second thought, let's just stay in and break in this closet you seem to love so much."

I licked my lips, the thought suddenly sounding like the best plan ever, when a throat cleared. Peeking around his bicep, I found Ryker standing closer to the doorway. He was dressed in tight jeans and a fitted shirt, the sleeves rolled up, and my mouth was suddenly parched.

"As much fun as that sounds, let's have dinner first." Ryker held out his hand, and I walked toward him, linking Cohen's hand in mine. When I reached him, Ryker's fingers entwined with my other hand, and I was suddenly the Oreo filling to a very hot man cookie.

"So, where are we going?" I asked as we started to head toward the garage, my voice cracking a little from the lust running through my body.

"That's a surprise, little hacker. You're going to have to be patient."

"I'm afraid that's a quality Fin has a shortage of," Cohen said, snorting to himself.

Huffing, I kept my comments to myself, afraid they'd make it worse if I rebuked their claims. Because Cohen wasn't wrong. I hated waiting for things. But I could do it, if it was to prove a point. Deciding to do just that, I smiled, concocting a plan for myself.

"Uh oh. She's got that look. Shit. I've activated bratty Fin. Quick, give her something to eat or something shiny."

I stopped, blinking at Cohen as I dropped both their hands and crossed my arms. "Um, what? I'm not a dog or a dragon!" I scrunched my eyebrows, trying to figure out where he was going with his comment.

Both guys stood silent for a second as they stared at me before falling into a fit of hysterics. Rolling my eyes, I began to walk forward, debating going to get Asa and Milo and having this date with them instead. When I entered the kitchen, it was lit with candles, and Asa and Milo stood in mock waiter uniforms. They were both smiling, but the instant they saw me, their eyes grew hungry, and their mouths parted a little.

"Man, I think we got the raw end of the deal. You look amazing, babe."

"Yeah, I want to change my role on this date," Milo said, pushing his glasses up.

Feeling appeased by their responses, I walked over to them, giving them each a hug and kiss. Once I was done, I turned and looked at the two troublemakers. They were standing together, hands practically touching, and I could feel the chemistry between them like electrical currents. Despite their obvious connection, both were focused on me, eyes hungry, their smiles contrite.

"Sorry, sweetheart. Please let us make it up to you with this evening we'd planned."

Nodding, I let Ryker and Cohen lead me to a table covered in a fancy linen tablecloth, candles, and fine china.

"Where did you get all of this?" I asked. We'd been moving all of our belongings into the house over the course of the week, but we hadn't had time to go and get things the house needed. Mainly because I'd been focused on getting my closet haven ready before anything else, but I didn't take the guys for ones to have dinnerware and cloth tablecloths.

"Sawyer brought it over earlier. She borrowed some of it from Aggie, and some are from my mom," Asa answered. "Now, for the rest of the meal, Milo and I will be your servers, not your boyfriends." Asa bowed and walked into the kitchen, bringing over trays of food that smelled delicious. "She also brought over some food that Ollie and Soren prepared."

"Remind me to thank her."

Ryker walked over and scooted my chair in

behind me, and the three of us sat down and began to eat. It was quiet as we enjoyed the meal, and while it was nice, it felt awkward.

"Okay, I thought this would be a good idea, but I'm beginning to see my flaw in this," Ryker said, pushing his plate back and getting up. "Come on. Let's eat dessert from the containers while sitting on the counters. Being too formal is making it weird."

Giggling, I took his hand and walked with him into the kitchen. Before I could hop up myself, Ryker lifted me onto the counter and handed me a spoon. Cohen leaned against the other side of me, and I was once again in the middle. I dipped my fork into the desert, getting a big scoop of whipped cream.

"You have something…" Cohen moved to point at my face, leaving a glob of whipped cream in his wake. "Oops, I better clean that up."

His tongue flicked out, trailing over my cheek, and I sucked in a breath. His eyes dropped to my tongue, and a second later, his mouth was on me as he kissed me passionately. I lost all thought as Cohen ravaged my mouth, so when hands began to trail up my legs, I jumped, pulling back. Ryker stood between them, his eyes hooded at half-mast as he took me in. His hands were hot on my skin, and I moved forward, wanting more contact.

"You sure? I know we're—"

"Ryker, touch me." His pupils fully dilated, and he pushed his palms up my legs, under my skirt. His fingers gripped my thighs, and I moaned at the contact. Cohen began to nibble on my neck, leaving little bites and sucks as he moved.

When he got to my ear, he whispered seductively. "Tell him what to do. It's sexy as fuck watching you take control, sweetheart. Tell him what you want, and I'll reward you."

My breath hitched, and I spread my legs open a little wider as my back arched. "Ryker, take off my panties."

Ryker's eyes jumped to mine, and I narrowed them at him. "Did I stutter?" He smiled, and I let out a little breath of relief I hadn't gone too far. Ryker was usually the dominant one, but it seemed like he wanted to submit to me. I'd never been in control this way before, but as Cohen urged me on, I found I liked it. If this was going to be the dynamic between the three of us, I was here for it.

Ryker's hand pushed my skirt the rest of the way up, my silk thong on display. I imagined the front displayed my wetness, my arousal leaking out onto my thighs already. Cohen began to move my top up, pulling it over my head as Ryker started to drag my panties down.

"Fuck, you're so sexy with your legs spread open

for me," Ryker said, staring at the space between my legs.

"Then show me. Kiss me there."

Cohen began to massage my breasts, tweaking my nipples through the lace and driving me wild. When Ryker's mouth hit my clit, my head fell back, and I locked my legs around him. His hands gripped me, and I knew I'd have marks tomorrow from how tight he held me to him. When his fingers plunged into me, I almost wept.

"You didn't tell him to do that," Cohen whispered, and I whimpered, not liking what that meant. I wanted him to do it even if I hadn't said it yet. Cohen gave me a pointed look, removing his hands from my tits. Sighing, I straightened up, peering down at the devilish man between my legs.

"I didn't give you permission to use your fingers. Cohen, show him what that means."

Since I was still new to figuring out what this was myself, I decided to call in the master. He gave me a smirk as I returned one, waiting for him to join in the fun. Ryker pulled his fingers out and looked to Cohen, waiting for whatever he was going to do. He snatched Ryker's fingers that were covered in my wetness and stuck them into his mouth, sucking them dry. Ryker and I both moaned, and I didn't know what sort of punishment this was since it was hot. When he was done with them, he pulled Ryker to him by his shirt, slamming their mouths together in a rough kiss that had me panting.

Pushing my own fingers into my wet pussy, I began playing with myself as I watched them. They seemed to get lost in one another, making me wetter with their connection and love, even if they were too afraid to admit it. Massaging my clit, I circled it roughly as I began to grow closer to my climax. When they pulled apart and stared at me with hungry eyes, I came, shuttering as my pussy tightened around the emptiness.

"Fuck, that was hot. I think it's time we give her something more. Playtime is over, little hacker."

Before I could respond, I was yanked off the counter by my hips and spun around. My bra was unclasped, falling to the surface. I could hear shuffling behind me, and the sound of a condom wrapper before the head of a cock was pressed into me from behind.

"Shit, Ry. You got your dick pierced!" Cohen exclaimed, catching me off guard as said dick was thrust into me. Arms wrapped around me, pulling me flush to a chest as he bent down to kiss me. When he pulled away, more of the cocky, flirty guy I knew was there, and I was happy to see him relaxing into himself and this.

His hands dropped to my hips, and I braced myself against the counter as he began to push into me harder, and I felt something I'd never experienced before. My breaths were heavy as he pistoned in and out, the smell of sex filling the space as our skin slapped together. I turned my head to the left, finding Cohen was now naked, his own cock in his hand as he stroked it, watching us.

He winked when he caught my gaze, bending down to kiss me. His free hand snaked down, rubbing my clit, and I detonated, unable to hold back the orgasm. White dots appeared in front of my eyes as I pulsed around Ryker, my body trembling.

"I'm coming," he roared, bracing himself against me as he pumped one last time. When he was done, he rested his head against my shoulder; our breathing synchronized as we tried to catch it.

"That… was… incredible…" I panted, making Ryker chuckle.

"It was. Now, round two." He kissed my shoulder before carefully pulling out, and I discovered what he meant. Cohen lifted me back to the counter, wrapping my legs around his waist as he plunged into me in one go. My body was sensitive from two orgasms already, so I held onto him, feeling every little move against my skin.

When a third orgasm began to creep up my spine,

my whole body tingled from my toes to my eyelashes.

"You are amazing, sweetheart. Hold on," Cohen whispered, kissing me. It didn't take much longer, and I fell apart in his arms. When I came to, a few minutes later, I knew that my worries were unfounded and that, once again, Sawyer had been right.

We were meant to be together, and I wouldn't let any more doubt or fear diminish our future because it was going to be a happy one.

ONE MONTH LATER

FINISHING UP MY CALL, I pushed my chair back and walked out of my office. Today had been long, but I was looking forward to the evening. Ryker and I were going to celebrate his starting work today. Everyone else was busy, so it would be the first time it would just be the two of us. Our relationship had flourished over the last month, and now that he was done with his physical therapy, he was cleared for duty. It had taken both Asa and me to convince him to come and work with Samson.

At first, he'd maintained he wanted some time off. But once everyone had started working and he was sitting at home alone, he quickly grew bored. He'd started some new hobbies, but after a week of basketweaving and gardening, he'd finally succumbed to our suggestion.

"Hey," I said, stepping into the fitness room. The new security recruits were all panting on the ground, and I had no doubt he'd given them a run for their money. Ryker turned at my voice, a smile on his handsome face. It was nice to see it there, and it only confirmed my intuition that he needed this job. He was good at it, and this way, it didn't come with all the stress running The Order did.

"Hello, boss man." He smirked at me as he walked closer. I took in his athletic form, noticing how his shorts fit him just right, hanging off his hips. His shirt was stretched across his chest, with a few damp spots where he'd sweated. While I appreciated Ryker in his suit, it was seeing him in his element that really got me going.

"You like that, don't you?" I asked, leaning against the wall by the door. It was a new experience for us both, me being in charge of him. I couldn't say I hated it.

"You done for the day?" I asked.

"Yep. I was about to head to the shower. Want to join?" Ryker asked, lifting his eyebrows. I took in every detail on his face. His eyes were hooded, but there was some vulnerability there too. Ryker stepped up next to me, his body heat surrounding me, and his rainforest and coffee smell tickled my nose. I itched to reach out to him and kiss him right there, but we were trying to keep it PG, at least in front of people. So, I took his hand, and we walked out of the gym together. I nodded at a few people, but no one even batted an eye, going on about their business.

Stepping into the private bathroom, I wasted no time shoving him against the door as I locked it. I trapped him between my arms. Ryker didn't even try to fight me, his eyes hungry as he leaned against me. I could feel his hardness as he rocked himself a little against me.

When we first got together, Ryker had been the aggressor, the one in charge of our dynamic. But since then, a lot had changed, and now, it was a battle between us to see who would give in each time we were together. It looked like today I was going to win.

"You were in your element today, weren't you?" I gripped his chin between my hands, and he nodded, licking his lips. "Answer."

"Yes," he said, his hot breath cascading over me, sending chills down my spine.

"Say, 'You were right, Cohen. You're a God among men.'" I smirked at him, waiting to see if he'd answer. The corner of his lip curved up, but he didn't say anything. Reaching down, I rubbed my hand over his cock, and he whimpered at the touch. "Want to try that again?" I asked, lifting my eyebrow.

"You were right, Cohen," he said between gritted teeth. A hiss left him as I stroked him again.

"I believe there was one more thing," I said, but this time, Ryker had had enough and surged up, sealing his lips to mine.

"Enough chit-chat. If you're not going to take control. I will."

Biting his lip for the insolence, I thrust my hand down his athletic shorts before he could retort, grabbing hold of his erect cock. Ryker sucked in a breath, breaking my grip on his mouth as his head hit the door.

"Now, what were you muttering about taking control?" Ever so slowly, I slid my hand up his length, rubbing my thumb over the piercing at the end and sending shivers down Ryker. Dropping to my knees, I pulled my prize free of his shorts and shoved them all the way down. I didn't waste any time, and I wrapped my lips around him, sucking him down to the back of my throat. Ryker's hands threaded through my hair, urging me to keep going.

I could feel him twitching in my mouth as I sucked him, swirling my tongue over the pierced tip. Grabbing his balls with my free hand, I fondled them as I took him further. I felt him give into the release, his legs tensing as his balls drew up, and he exploded his salty cum down my throat. Licking my lips, I stood and began to undress while Ryker recovered.

Turning on the shower, I glanced back at him as he rested against the door, the blood returning to his brain. "I'm not done with you," I cooed, walking over and grabbing his throat as I slammed my lips to his. Ryker trembled beneath me, submitting completely to me as I took what I wanted.

Breaking the kiss, I walked over to the shower and beckoned him to follow. The shower was tiled and open, with a bench to one side and four shower heads. The water rained down from every direction, and I pointed for him to take the bench. Ryker didn't hesitate as I grabbed some lube, directing all the shower heads away from me.

When I looked back at him, his ass in the air, I stopped, not believing what I saw.

"Did you…?" I mumbled, lost for words.

Ryker glanced over his shoulder, a smirk on his face. "Wear this all day? Yep."

Peering at me from between his ass cheeks was a black butt plug. The sight made me harder if that was even possible. "Shit," I cursed, stroking myself.

I walked forward, reverently massaging his ass cheeks as I took in the sight. It said a lot for Ryker to do this, and I knew no matter what, our relationship would survive anything else. Taking hold of the plug, I gently pulled it out, his hole gaping as it waited to be filled. Ryker moaned at the movement, and I took some lube and dripped it around him.

Gripping his hips, I pushed in easier than I'd ever done before, sliding home. We both cursed when I bottomed out, and I stood there for a second as I breathed, trying not to erupt before I got to enjoy myself.

Slowly, I pulled back, feeling him tremble around me as I moved. "Fuck, Ry. You made me so hard doing that."

"Good," he wheezed out between pants, his hands braced on the bench.

We didn't say much else, both of us too lost to the pleasure coursing through us. My balls were tingling with the need to come, but I wasn't ready yet. It felt so good to just fuck him.

Ryker whimpered, the sound pained, and I knew I couldn't wait much longer. Pulling his torso up, I stopped and tilted his head back so I could kiss him.

"Ready?" I asked, and he nodded.

Tightening my grip, I pushed forward, loving how easily I slid back into him. Giving one more thrust, I roared as I came, my cum filling him.

When I could think again, I slowly pulled out,

helping him to stand. Ryker turned to me, clasping my face in a tender hold, staring into my eyes.

"I love you, Cohen. I'm not afraid to admit it anymore, and I just wanted you to know that."

My throat felt dry as I tried to find the words. I blinked, the water hitting me now that I'd moved to the side. When I didn't say anything, he gave me an understanding look.

"I get it. I don't have the best track record—"

Shushing him with a kiss, I drew back, shaking my head. "No, that's not it. I'm just surprised you said it first. Finley totally won the bet. I love you too, Ryker."

He half laughed and frowned at my words. Shaking his head, he peered at me, his eyes lighter. "How about we finish up and go and have that date we'd planned? And maybe there will be time for round two?"

Smiling, we quickly rinsed, turning off the shower and dressing in record time. When we stepped outside, the sun was beginning to set. I leaned my head back, having missed the sun more than I realized when we'd been at The Order. Now, every chance I got, I soaked it in, even if only at the end of the day.

"Yeah, that's the good stuff. I'd gotten so used to being underground that I'd forgotten what the real sun was like. Those vitamin D lamps just aren't the same. Plus, you just can't mimic this view."

I peered over, nodding. "Yeah, I was thinking the same."

"You know, I think our subconscious tries to protect us by making us forget how perfect some things are. It's the only reason I can imagine for how I forgot how amazing you were. I tried to forget so I wouldn't be miserable each day."

My cheeks blushed as we started walking. "I'm not perfect. Far from it. But I'm glad we're here now."

Ryker squeezed my hand, and we headed back to the house, ready to live out our lives with the people we loved and the family we'd created.

I hope you've enjoyed Finley's story. It was one I knew I wanted to tell from the beginning. I think it's important for us all to find our own way; however, we choose to do that. Finley is strong in so many ways, but it takes her a while to see. Hopefully, through her story, you found some strength within yourself.

While her story was shorter, I love the happy ending that she got with her guys. Maybe there will be more at some point, but for now, the door is closed on these characters.

Now, if you know me, I can't ever fully say goodbye, which is why they will pop in now and again in the new series, Lux Brumalis, that will be coming next. Did you catch the girls talking about the characters at the end? Henley, Dax, Fletcher, and Reed will be our next group of characters to fall in love with. I can't wait to see what story they unfold.

I'm forever grateful to Emma and Megan for being there with me through all the edits. Seriously, your love for all the characters keeps me going. Hopefully, Ryker getting stabbed was rewarding enough for you, Megan.

Thanks to Lindsay for being able to provide feedback on a tight deadline. Your insight helps me remember the story and why I love it.

To all my readers, thank you for sticking around for another one. If you loved it or hated it, I love seeing your reviews, edits, and TikToks. They make me remember why I write on the nights when I wonder if anyone cares. So, thank you for loving these characters.

To my husband, I love you. Thanks for the endless supply of Sunkist Zero to keep my going.

Dangerous Lies

Dangerous Vows

Reckless (Cami's Novella)

Relentless (Nat's Novella)

Dangerous Love

TATTOOED HEARTS DUET

Tattooed Hearts Completed Duet

Riddled Deceit (Part 1)

Smudged Lines (Part 2)

Open Road

MUSIC CITY DIARIES

Beautiful Agony

Beautiful Envy

FRIENDSHIP & LYRICS

Vibing: A Vacation Rom-Com

SINNERS FAIRYTALES

(standalone)

Pride

About the Author

Kris Butler writes under a pen name to have some separation from her everyday life. Never expecting to write a book, she was surprised when an author friend encouraged her to give it a try and how much she enjoyed it. Having an extensive background in mental health, Kris hopes to normalize mental health issues and the importance of talking about them with her characters and books. Kris is a southern girl at heart but lives with her husband and adorable furbaby somewhere in the Midwest. Kris is an avid fan of Reverse Harem and hopes to add a quirky and new perspective to the emerging genre. If you enjoyed her book, please consider leaving a review. You can contact her the following ways and follow Kris's journey as a new author on social media.

Join my newsletter

Join my group